No More Thuggin

Anointed Inspirations Publishing
Presents

D1414982

No More Thuggin

By

Jenica Johnson and Denora M. Boone

Published by Anointed Inspirations Publishing

www.anointedinspirationspublishing.org

Note: This is a work of fiction. Names, characters, places

and incidents either are products of the author's

imagination or are used fictitiously. Any resemblance to

actual events or locales or persons, living or dead, is entirely coincidental

Anointed Inspirations Publishing is currently accepting Christian Fiction submissions. For consideration please send manuscripts to

Anointedinspirationspublishing@gmail.com

Connect with Jenica:

Facebook:
https://www.facebook.com/jenica.johnson.5

Instagram: fearfully_wonderfully_me

Twitter: @authorjenica

Connect with Denora:

Facebook:
https://www.facebook.com/AuthorDenora

Instagram: @mzboone81

Twitter: @mzboone27

From the Authors

We ALWAYS thank God and our families because without them these books wouldn't be possible!

But this book goes out to our READERS!! The support that each of you continue to show us means more than you know. So since you all asked for it we have delivered! #AIP is a family and you all are a part of it. We all we got!

Please leave your reviews and let us know how we did!

Love Jenica and Denora

Chasiti

I was huge! Being a big girl already God knew I didn't need to gain any more weight but the way this pregnancy was set up I was miserable. My feet were constantly swollen, my nose looked big as ever, and I didn't even want my own husband touching me. Not that he wanted to anyway.

Gavon had been real distant lately and I didn't know if it was because of me, the ministry he was now in charge of, or something else. He never came home after 7pm which I appreciated but when he got there he was so tired and snappy. Most times he would eat the dinner I prepared, play a little with our daughter Jean'nae, find out how my day went and then it was lights out by ten.

Once Mama Jean passed it just felt like he had taken on the weight of the world and I understood where he was coming from. It was like when she was alive she made life seem so much easier. Though she wasn't there in the natural we constantly felt her spirit daily and that gave me some comfort. Especially during this high risk pregnancy.

Gavon, Jr was a handful already and he wasn't even here yet. I can only imagine how he would be once he entered this world and in a few short weeks we would soon find out.

I had just dropped Jean'nae off to daycare and was on my way back home when my phone rang with an unknown number. Hitting the hands free button on my steering wheel I answered as I made my way down the expressway.

"Hello?" I answered. It never bothered me picking up unknown calls since our credit was good and we paid all of our bills on time. But something about this one before I answered had me feeling uneasy.

"Chasiti?" the woman said. I hadn't heard her voice in almost three years and although I didn't hate her, I still didn't want to talk to her.

"Chardonnay? Well how have you been?" I did my best to sound chipper so she couldn't pick up on the hidden attitude I was trying my best to hide.

"I'm good. How are you feeling these days?" she asked me. For some reason she sounded unsure about this call and now my curiosity was piqued.

"Just fine thanks."

I had heard that a while after she had given her life to The Lord she moved away to another state and she had even gotten married. I didn't do too much gossiping so never did I ask where because I really didn't care one way or another.

I honestly had forgiven her the day I stopped Gavon from killing her I felt like my good deed was done. There was no need to stay in touch after that and it was best that we all took the time we needed to heal from the whole ordeal. Moving on was imperative for he and I and this call was making me wonder if she had moved on or not.

"So what do I owe this pleasure of a phone call?" I asked hoping she would get to the point. By now I was hungry and a chicken, egg, and cheese biscuit from McDonald's and a frozen lemonade from Chick-fil-a was calling my name something loud.

I giggled inwardly thinking of how Mama Jean never called a chicken by its actual name but she always called it a 'yard bird'. That old woman was a mess. Had she still been here she probably would have fussed out Chardonnay then hung up on her as soon as she heard her voice.

"Well I know that you're almost ready to deliver but-." she started before I cut her off.

"Wait. How do you know I'm about to have a baby?" Something wasn't right and I was about to catch a serious attitude.

"Um that's what I wanted to meet with you about. I've been seeing Gavon and I thought you should know." She said sounding uneasy.

Now I don't know what the enemy thought when he came up with this cockamamie attack but pregnant or not I was about to get to the bottom of this. What in the world did she mean by 'she has been seeing Gavon'?

All I could see was red as I pulled into the parking lot of Chick-fil-a and parked. I knew my pressure was up because these Braxton Hicks were kicking in full force. If Chardonnay thought she was coming back into our lives to mess up what we had established then she had another thing coming. She wanted a fight? Then a fight she would get.

"Where are you?" I asked as I focused on getting my breathing under control.

"I was about to stop and get something to eat before heading to my realtor and get the keys for my new apartment, I just moved back to Savannah." She said. You could have knocked my big behind over with a feather at that bit of news.

"I'm at the Chick-fil-a on Pooler Parkway. Can you meet me here?" I asked her.

I needed God to intervene because I was getting myself worked up and didn't even know why. For all I know she could have been meeting him with her husband for counseling or something. But if that was the case then why hadn't he let me know?

"Oh that's perfect. I was just about to stop and get me a frozen lemonade before I headed over to McDonald's. These pregnancy cravings are killer this go round."

"You're pregnant?" I asked.

I swear to God I'm going to jail at 37 weeks if the next words out of her mouth were the same ones I was thinking.

"Um. Gavon didn't tell you about me huh?" she said having the nerve to sound sad.

"No."

By now livid would be an understatement as I noticed a newer model Lincoln Navigator pull up to my right and park. Chardonnay looked into my eyes with hers filled with sadness and the phone still to her ear while she opened her driver's side door.

I couldn't lie she was looking flawless and I saw why Gavon used to mess with her back then. Besides being ratchet had she carried herself back then like she does now they may have worked one day. Just that thought alone made my stomach feel tighter but the sight before me made my chest tighten as well.

"We really need to talk then." She said still looking at me through the window as my eyes left her face and landed on her big round belly.

If that wasn't enough to send me under, the dampness I began to feel between my legs sure would. Fine time for my water to break huh?

Alvin

I watched as my son paced the floor of the hospital room while my daughter-in-law slept peacefully in the hospital bed. Her labor had stalled for the second time and I could tell Gavon was nervous. He reminded me so much of myself and it brought back memories of when Danielle was in labor with him and Mama Jean tried comforting me.

"Boy sit down." I chuckled.

"I can't Pops. Chas didn't go through this with Jean'nae and everyone seems to be so calm about it. This can't be normal." He said looking just like I did over thirty years ago.

"Must be something bout little boys named Gavon." I said with a smile on my face. I couldn't help but to be amused by the look on his face so I continued.

"Son this was exactly what you did to your mother. Why do you think you are the only child? Your mother went through twenty six hours of labor and four stalls." I

informed him.

"Well this is it for me too! Somebody come get this

baby out of me I have to push!" Chasiti said startling the

both of us. Gavon didn't know if he should go to her side or

run out the door to get the nurse. He was running around

looking like a chicken with his head cut off.

Not saying word but giving Chasiti a look asking

her to calm down I placed my sleeping two year old

granddaughter Jean'nae on the couch beside me and moved

towards the bed. Gavon was right comical but I understood

how he felt. I pushed the call button on the side of the bed

and told the nurse what was going on.

I was a little confused at the voice that I heard on

the other end but I knew who it was immediately and that

caused a smile to spread across my face. Gavon may have

missed it but Chasiti certainly did not. That girl never

missed a beat and the look on her face let me know that she was expecting an answer from me.

Before I could give her one though a contraction ripped through her body and my hand was the closest for her to grab. I knew I should have moved out of the way but I was too slow. The door pushed open and in came the doctor followed by Chasiti's grandfather Rev. Rockmore and one of the most beautiful women I have seen in a long time.

"Let's get this show on the road Mrs. Cunningham." Dr. Brantley said as she got in position in front of the bed.

The pain from Chasiti holding my hand had subsided as I watched her nurse move around the room getting everything situated for my grandson's arrival. The way her short hair framed her face with soft curls made her big bright eyes seem to shine even more. I like this look on her. The last time had seen her she had long Havana twist that made her look even younger than she already looked.

No More Thuggin

Her name was Marisa and I had met her a few years ago before I was released. She had come to visit one of the other inmates. Mama Jean was there that day and she caught me sneaking a few glances at her but she didn't say a word. Just gave me a knowing smile. I was home a few months and had taken a trip to Atlanta to make a delivery. Chasiti's grandfather Reverend Rockmore had pulled some strings with Coca Cola and since I was exonerated they couldn't use my history against me.

Anyway I was making a delivery and I bumped into her at one of the stores. I knew that if I ever saw her gorgeous face again I would never forget it. I didn't bother asking the inmate she was visiting who she was just because I didn't want to offend him. I figured that if she had been a relative maybe she would send word back to me. It never came but I didn't forget her.

When she walked up to me and asked me why I never asked for her number or information from her uncle I was shocked. Not only because she was waiting on me to reach out but because her uncle looked like he was the same age as her.

Since that day we had kept in contact and even tried the long distance relationship thing. Neither of us was feeling it, so she transferred to the hospital here in Savannah to build a relationship with me. I had yet to tell Gavon about her because she was so far away and I knew that he was still holding on to his mother. Just getting me back into his life and reconciling our relationship, I felt like this news may have him hostile towards me again. It wasn't like I was cheating on his mother and he wasn't the only one who missed her. It wasn't a day that went by I didn't think of her and I don't think there ever will be.

That's how I know Marisa is the one. I told her everything good and bad about me and she was so considerate of my feelings. When she told me that she would never try to replace Danielle she only wanted to be who God created her to be for me, I felt like I had a winner. Now if only I could get over the fear of what my son would think I would be a happy man. I would have a beautiful, intelligent, God fearing woman by my side, my son and grandbabies along with his wife who I adored, and making an honest living.

But the way he was watching me watch Marisa with a mean mug on his face I knew this wouldn't be easy. Not by a long shot.

Gavon

After ten hours of labor Dr. Brantley decided to give Chasiti a C-section. I didn't want her to have one but my sons heart rate started dropping and Chasiti's blood pressure starting elevating. After they prepped her and got her on the table, I sat at her head as she looked at me with a slight smile. I could tell something was bothering her but she was in the moment and now wasn't the time to talk about it.

The sound of the suctions made Chasiti sick so the anesthesiologist gave her something for nausea. No soon after the pulling and tugging I heard the cries of my son. I wanted to hop up and see him but I knew I could cross over into the sterilized area. Dr. Brantley placed Gavon Jr. over the top of the barrier and Chasiti started crying. He had his eyes closed tight but he was hollering so we knew he was okay. I wiped her tears and kissed her forehead.

"Alright dad, you ready to cut the cord?" the nurse asked.

I hopped up so fast because I was so ready to check my son out. Gavon Jr. was huge, his pale skin had a white substance on it that looked like cheese. The nurse wiped as much off as she could before I was able to cut his cord. He had his whole fist in his mouth, as much as Chasiti ate, I knew he couldn't be hungry. The nurse weighed Gavon Jr. and placed his pamper on and wrapped him in his blanket. When she placed him in my arms all I could do was stare at him. God had to really trust me to bless me with two kids. I wanted to make sure that I was a good father but somedays it felt like I was failing at it.

I walked Lil Gee over to Chasiti so she could see him. Sitting back on the stool I rolled over to her head while the doctor finished sowing her up.

"Oh my goodness he is huge. How much did he weigh?"

"He was 8 pounds even. That's all that McDonald's and Chic fil-a you been eating," I laughed at her.

She didn't laugh back so that let me know something was really wrong. I placed Gavon Jr.'s face to Chasiti's face so she could kiss him and he opened his eyes. When he opened them, they reminded me of Mama Jean's eyes.

"Bae look at him. Who does he look like?" I asked Chasiti.

"He look like Mama Jean with those eyes," she said.

"Alright mama and daddy we need to get him in the warmer. They are about to place Chasiti in recovery for about an hour or two and then she will be in the room. You're welcome to come to the nursery anytime as long as you have your band on," the nurse said before taking my son out of my arms.

No More Thuggin

On my way to Chasiti's room I saw my Pops leaning all over the nurse's station flirting with the same nurse that was helping Chasiti during labor. I hope he didn't think he was just going to continue to flirt in my face like it was cool. I cleared my throat so he would know I had seen him.

I waited for two hours before Chasiti had finally come out of recovery. Now that she was in her room sleeping peacefully, I was able to pull my iPad out and check some of my emails. I did street ministry on certain days of the week and today was one of those days. I hated to cancel but I wasn't about to leave Chasiti and my first born son up here by themselves. The nurse brought me a few blankets so I would be comfortable and checked to see if we needed anything else before her shift ended. After telling her thank you and confirming we were good I stretched out on the uncomfortable tiny sofa when my Pops walked in.

"Aye son I'm bout to get out of here. I'll be by tomorrow and bring Lil Gee some pampers and some more stuff. I'm going to stop by and pick Jean'nae up from Rev before I call it a night. Do you or Chas need anything?"

"Nah, we straight," I said without looking up. I was hoping he heard the hostility in my voice but I guess he didn't care because he shrugged his broad shoulders and walked out.

Once I was able to answer the few emails I had in my inbox I decided to close my eyes for a while since Chasiti was finally resting. I was well aware that sleep wasn't going to come easy once we got home so I had better enjoy it while I could.

A few hours had passed before I woke up to my wife nursing my son. The sight before me put a smile on my face and I couldn't help the feeling of my heart swelling with pride.

I sat up and stretched before I got up off the tiny sofa and went over to sit on the edge of her bed.

"He's perfect Gavon."

"I know. Lil dude got a head full of curls too. We got to cut that mess off though or dread it up."

"No you will not dread my baby's hair up. Neither will you be cutting it until he is at least a year old."

"Whatever Chas. Aye did you see Pop's eyes bout to fall out staring at that nurse today?" I asked Chasiti.

"Yea and I thought it was cute."

"There is nothing cute about no old man trying to flirt like he's in his twenties. He's too old to be carrying on like that."

"Cut it out cause you sound crazy. I think it's good for Pops to try and get back out there after all of these years. He's not young but he certainly isn't dead yet. He deserves to find someone that he can settle down with. He can't keep being lonely Gavon."

"Man whatever I'm not trying to hear what you talking bout."

This topic of conversation had been the norm for us lately when it came to my father dating. I would notice how he would flirt with other women sometimes when we were hanging out and I even called him on it a few times. What upset me the most was that he would brush those ladies off but told me he had his eye on someone else.

"You are being selfish Gee and you know it," Chasiti said bringing me from my thoughts. "You know what lets just drop it because I don't even want to get worked up right now. Not only did I just have a baby but I'm dealing with something of my own."

"What's wrong and why didn't you tell me something was bothering you? Talk to me bae." I scooted closer to her.

"No I need to wait and see what God reveals to me before I jump ahead of myself. It'll come to the light," she said as she frowned and adjusted the baby over her shoulder to burp him. Something in her tone let me know it was serious but I wouldn't press the issue. Like she said whatever it was it would all come to the light soon enough.

"So have you decided what you want to do about getting some help around the house?" I asked her.

"I can handle it," she said burping Lil Gee.

"I figured you were going to say that so I got my cousin Shenita coming to help." I told her reaching over for her to pass me my son.

His eyes were opened and it looked like he was trying to focus but his little eyes kept crossing. When we had Nae and her eyes did that for the first time I almost cried because I thought she was going to be cockeyed. After the nurses and doctors told me that was normal I calmed down. The last thing I wanted was for anyone to say my kids eyes were cocked like a pistol.

"Oh well as long as it's my girl Shenita then I'm good."

"Yea, she's about the only one I can trust around our kids besides my old man and yours. If it's one thing that Mama Jean taught me coming up it was not to let so many people into my inner circle. She said that it could always be the ones the closest to me that could hurt me so I had to use my gift of discernment.

"I can deal with Shenita's crazy behind. It's like having a younger Mama Jean in the house except with an accent," Chasiti laughed.

Shenita would always come down to spend the summers with us when we were younger. She was my uncle Reno's daughter but lived with her mother Precious in New Orleans. When she came for Mama Jean's funeral she told me if I ever needed her to call and she would be on the next flight. When I noticed how tired Chasiti had become around her sixth month of pregnancy, I knew she was going to need a little more help. Besides I think Chasiti wanted some company anyway, because I was never home.

Ministry had become full time for me since I accepted and walked into my calling and purpose. If I could hug the block when I was out there doing me with no complaints then I could surely go harder for God. Not only that but I knew that Shenita would get Jean'nae's spoiled behind in check too. Chasiti tried but it was all my fault that Jean'nae was a little brat. She was a daddy's girl at heart.

Chasiti

I was a woman that didn't like to confront an issue until I had all of my facts together. Chardonnay hadn't called back, but just as sure as she does I'm asking her every question I could think of. When my water broke that day in the parking lot of the restaurant she left as soon as the EMTs arrived. I wanted so bad to get to the bottom of what was going on but the way those contractions started hitting me I couldn't focus on her and what could possibly be going on with my husband.

The baby and I been home for three days now and Gavon was stuck to me like glue. He was able to put some of the things in the ministry in the hands of the assistant pastor as well as my grandfather. They made it easier for him to be able to take care of us first so that we could get situated and in a routine. Shenita was supposed to fly in today and I was sure that once she got settled he would be gone as usual because he knew she would be a big help to me.

It was a little odd though because today he was acting really strange. He kept checking his phone every few minutes and flipping it face down so I couldn't see the screen. I had figured out that instead of the ringer being on he had turned it to vibrate. The only time he did that was when we were in church. Neither of us ever turned the ringers off of our phones because we never knew when someone would be in need. Once we stepped into the position at church we made sure to be available to anyone who may have needed us.

I acted like I wasn't paying attention but I was downloading it all to my memory bank so that when the time came to confront him I would be ready.

Looking up from the sofa as I nursed Lil Gee I heard our front door open and I could hear some wheels rolling across the hardwood floor.

"Hey baybee," Shenita walked in popping her gum. "Y'all must feel safe huh? Leaving the door unlocked."

Shenita stood about 5'9" with a thick frame. Her skin was a pretty chocolate color and her full lips and dark eyes complimented her skin tone. She wore her hair in a nice curly style with some deep purple lipstick. That lipstick was her signature. Her New Orleans accent was so strong sometimes I had to ask her what she said twice. She put you in the mind of the rising star Supa out of New Orleans. They favored one another and if you closed your eyes you would swear they were one in the same.

"What's up Shenita," Gavon walked up and gave her a big hug. If it was one person in his family that he was as close to as Mama Jean it was definitely Shenita. The stories he would tell of their summers together would have me balled up in laughter.

"Gavon I ain't stuntin you where them baybee's at? Well looka here," she said walking up and standing over

Lil Gee once she knew we were in the room. "Did y'all make this baybee or Mama Jean? Chasiti what you did guh he don't look nothing like your behind. Von must have made you mad the whole nine months huh?"

"I guess I just carried him." I laughed as I handed the baby over to her.

"You dang gone right that's all you did. What y'all got to eat I'm hungry," Shenita walked in the kitchen carrying Lil Gee snuggly in her arms.

"Bae I'm about to run off real quick I'll be back for dinner," Gavon said kissing my lips and making sure he had everything he needed before heading out the door.

Shenita came back in the living room with a plate of warmed up spaghetti with her gum stuck to the side of the plate. Shenita knew she loved her some gum and popping it loud was a must.

"Y'all ain't got no paper cups round here? Gee done became too high classed for me, he know all we use is paper products."

"Shenita if you don't get a cup and hush." I laughed at her as she continued to stuff her mouth all while holding the baby in her arm and smacking loudly. Jean'nae came running in the living room full speed ahead bouncing right up on the sofa.

"Jean'nae what did I tell you about bouncing on the sofa like that. I know you see your brother sleeping. You're going to wake him up," I told her.

"See that's why I'm here because she need a whopping. What you call yourself doing is not working cause look at her lil behind she still bouncing. Jean'nae get down from that sofa befo' I bust you in the back," Shenita yelled.

Jean'nae quickly stopped jumping and sat right on down. I had never seen this little girl move so fast in my life especially when she got in trouble. Normally she would mumble under her breath or act like she didn't hear you but not this time. Shenita may have been just what I needed to get my little spoiled diva under control.

"See you got to get a lil crazy with them sometimes," Shenita said while giving Jean'nae a crucial side eye daring her to move from that spot.

"You are crazy," I laughed. "What have you been up too?"

"Girl the usual trying to get somebody to marry my crazy behind. You know don't no man want a strong woman like me from the N.O. cause I'll read him his rights, ya kno."

"Girl marriage is hard work."

"Wait now. Why you sound like that doh?" she asked still smacking on her meal. I knew that I could throw down in the kitchen but the way she was eating it made me want to get some of my own.

"I think your cousin is cheating on me Nita," I told her as I watched her eyes get big and she dropped her fork into the bowl. By the look on her face I knew that she was shocked and under normal circumstances her reaction would be comical but this was not a laughing matter.

"Hole on nah. After all the hard work he put in to get you Chasiti I don't think he would do that," Shenita said with assurance.

"Well tell me why the day I went into labor Chardonnay had called me and asked if we could meet up. We were both in the area and when she pulled up and got out I saw that she was pregnant. She even told me that she needed to talk to me about your cousin because she was seeing him," I informed her.

"Oh no baybee we got to go see bout ha. Where she at doh? I can't stand her nappy headed self. Is she still bald round the edges?" Shenita asked with her face balled up.

"Shenita stop," I said laughing.

"I just wanna kno."

"I haven't seen her so I don't know. I hate to tell you this but if I find out Gavon cheating on me with her, you can take him back to New Orleans with you because I'm not going to deal with it."

"Guh be quiet Gee ain't doing nothing with that girl."

"I hope you're right," I said not too sure that I was in agreement with her at this moment.

"I'm about to take Lil Gee to his room and get this little jumping bean down for a nap. Look at her, she so do-do now that I made her behind sit still," Shenita said.

"Do-do?" I asked confused. If Shenita was going to be here assisting me then I was going to have to go online and find some New Orleans translations to decipher her dialogue.

"It means she's sleepy. Lord I see I'm gone have to speak proper English this trip. Anyway gone nah so you can rest. It's only been three days so go get in the bed. I'll cook us up some good ole creole food tonight baybee. You eat mudbugs?"

"Ewww what is that!" I shrieked almost waking up the baby and causing Jean'nae to jump.

"Crawfish guh."

Instead of responding all I could do was scrunch my nose and mouth up and shake my head no.

"Oh you are in for a treat. Gone nah and get rested."

I got up from the sofa slowly because my incision was still tender and I didn't want to bust it open. I made sure to grab my phone so I could charge it while I was sleep. I was so thankful that Shenita was here because I was in need of some serious rest I didn't want to seem like I was lazy. No matter how my body felt I still had a responsibility to uphold so I made sure to always be up before Gavon to make sure I was still fulfilling my wife duties.

He didn't like the fact that I was always up running behind Jean'nae or making sure the house was in order. So many times he told me to let him handle it but I would ignore him. If he was out doing the work of the Lord then the least I could do was make sure home was taken care of.

It never failed that he would fuss about him doing it but as soon as I didn't handle it neither did he. Ministry drained him some days and when he came in he would hit the bed. So since he wasn't doing it I refused to let my house get nasty just because I had a new baby.

Pulling my cover back I climbed into our comfortable king sized bed while making sure to adjust my pillows just right. I still couldn't fully lay down like normal because trying to get up from a low position made the pain worse. All I could do was sigh in relief because this was the first time since being home that I was able to just get in my bed and close my eyes without Lil Gee on my breast or Jean'nae begging for something and it felt so good! Before

No More Thuggin

I knew it my heavy eyes were losing the battle and I let

sleep take over.

No More Thuggin

Chardonnay

I knew that when I called Chasiti the other day that it may or may not have gone well. Knowing what I knew about her, it not going well seemed the most plausible. The last thing that I wanted to happen was for her to get as upset as she did and I could clearly see the hurt expression on her face when she saw me get out of my car.

I know that I should have checked up on her to make sure that everything was ok with her and the baby but from the looks of it she clearly wasn't in the mood.

The last time I had seen Chasiti it was when I gave my life over to God and let Jesus into my heart. That was one of the hardest decision I had ever had to make in my life but it was worth it. After the night Gavon almost took my life when he found out I was the reason he was stabbed and I was the last person that made his grandmother upset before she died, he was dead set on taking my life for hers.

I knew he had blamed me and in a way I blamed myself a little too. Had I not been so extra about him not wanting anything to do with me anymore and moving on to Chasiti maybe Mama Jean would have still been here. My life was spared and I had God and Chasiti to thank for that. That girl showed me a different side of her that day so the last thing that I wanted to do was hurt her. But once again here I was causing pain in someone's life and it just happened to be the same person.

"I'm about to head out baby. Call me and let me know how your appointment goes," my husband Kendrick told me before kissing me on my cheek and walking out of the front door. He didn't even give me time to respond but I really didn't care. Things between us haven't been good for a long time and that was one of the reasons that I invited Gavon back into my life.

I rubbed my swollen belly as I felt my daughter kick. She was kicking me so hard from the inside I thought she would burst through at any moment.

"Little girl if you don't stop kicking me so hard," I scolded like she could really understand me right before my phone dinged indicating I had a new message.

Von: What's going on?

Things weren't right and I knew these feelings may make things worse but right then I needed him in order to feel some sense of comfort and he was the only one that could help me get it.

Me: Kendrick just left so are you on the way?

Von: As soon as my cousin Shenita gets here I'll be on the way.

Me: Hurry up I really need to see you.

Von: Don't worry I'm coming.

After responding to a few more text to Gavon I got up and made my way into the kitchen. It felt like I was eating every ten minutes with this little girl. I guess she was making up for the many meals she had caused me to miss being sick in my first trimester. Gavon had told me that Chasiti went through the same thing so he gave me some of the home remedies that worked for her.

Standing in the door of the refrigerator I couldn't see anything that I wanted to eat that was fast. Suddenly I got a taste for some Chinese food and for some strange reason that craving made my mind drift to Gavon. That was something that we had always enjoyed together so as I picked up the phone to place the order I made sure to order him his favorite as well.

As soon as I had ended the call there was a knock at the door. Instantly I knew who it was and I began to get nervous. Whenever I was around this man it was like he could see into my innermost being and often times that scared me a tad bit.

No More Thuggin

I made sure my hair was in place and my clothes were straight. Today I was rocking a big curly twist out and as usual my face was beat to perfection. Since I had turned my life around some I had let my colorful weave go and embraced my natural hair.

I never realized how bad those sew ins had made my hair unhealthy and understood why Mama Jean would always go off on me about having no edges. They were straight gone and I had no one to blame for it but myself.

Even my wardrobe had changed significantly. I had started to dress the way I wanted people to look at me and that was not the same mindset I had all of these years ago. I thought dressing provocatively was appealing to me but it only made them want my body and I gave it to them. Once I started building my relationship with God He showed me that I worth way more than what I was giving off and I wanted to change for the better. Too bad Kendrick didn't feel the same way.

Another round of knocks on the door brought me out of my daydream and I rushed over to open it. Standing there with his back turned was my first love. I know I may have had a funny way of showing y love for Gavon back then but now that I was being honest with myself I could no longer deny it.

The dreads he sported had gotten about four inches longer and I could tell that he had just gotten them retwisted. I knew Chasiti had done them because she made sure to take care of home. That was something else I admired about her.

Just by looking at Gavon you would never be able to tell that he was a minister unless you heard him preach at church or knew him personally. The way he dressed you would think that he was still in the streets heavy. He was forever rocking some jeans and Jordans and the jewelry he wore could compete with any of the pieces the dope boys wore. Gavon was still fine to me and it wasn't until he spoke that I realized I was standing in my door with it wide open right along with my mouth.

Get thee behind me Satan! I thought to myself.

So are you going to make me just stand here or can I come in?"

"Oh. Sorry," I said embarrassed.

He gave me that killer smile that he carried around but I noticed that it didn't reach his eyes. Something was bothering him and I already knew what it was.

"You want anything to drink?"

"Nah I'm straight. I just wanted to talk to you before I headed over to the church."

The way he said that made me uneasy and this was a topic that I knew bothered him.

"So what's going on?" I wanted to know.

"Char we have to stop this. As right as I thought this was in the beginning I'm not so sure anymore."

This conversation was going into a different direction than I had initially thought. I couldn't understand what he was getting at and I was sure my face displayed it. If he was telling me that he could no longer meet up with me that was something that I didn't know how to take. He was really my saving grace.

"What do you mean?"

"I mean we have to stop sneaking behind her back before she starts doing any more assuming than she already is."

"You think she knows?" I asked worried. This was the last thing that I needed.

"I'm not sure but the way she looks at me isn't the same anymore. When we started this I admit it was my idea but we were both needing something from each other that she nor Kendrick could give us."

That was one thing he was definitely right about. When we moved back to Savanah I had hoped that

Kendrick would get his act together but it felt like he only got worse. He was so sloppy with the other women that he didn't even care anymore. I knew he felt like he was all I had and to an extent he was but I needed more and the only person that I knew could help me get it was Gavon.

"Maybe it's just her hormones raging."

Shrugging his shoulders he ran his hand over his face before speaking again.

"Pops may have found a new woman."

I knew this was going to come up eventually because this was one of our regular conversations. He felt like his father was moving too fast since getting out of jail and I understood where he was coming from. I knew he wanted me to listen and give him some advice so I always did my best.

"When did this happen?"

"I don't know but it couldn't have been too long ago. I just found out when she was Chasiti's nurse while she was in labor."

"How does Chasiti feel about it?"

"She is still hashtag team Alvin. I just don't see how she could accept this like it's ok." He said getting up and walking over to the living room window.

I could tell this was frustrating to him and in a way it made me feel the same way. As much as Alvin claimed to love Danielle for him to move on after only being out a while I didn't understand it. And Chasiti not siding with her husband wasn't right. No matter what I felt that she should stand by her man come hell or high water especially with something like this. Unlike with my situation, her husband actually loved her.

Walking over to stand behind him I placed my hand on his back. I was so much in his space that my baby bump touched him. Feeling him relax under my touch pushed all thoughts of me speaking with Chasiti to the back of my mind.

"It's ok. I understand and I agree that the way you are feeling is justified. Both Alvin and Chasiti need to get a grip and understand what they are doing is wrong."

Turning to face me the look in his eyes told me that he appreciated me being on his side. This was new for the both of us because I had always been so against him while we were together.

The intensity of how he was looking at me made the air I was breathing in seem to get stuck in my throat. I could feel my palms getting sweaty as he placed his left hand on my cheeks and leaned into me slowly. Both of our breath had become labored and my body felt hot. Right before our lips connected his phone rang and by the ringtone I knew that it was Chasiti.

Gavon reached into his pocket and hit the ignore button and pulled back.

"Let's get this over before she calls back."

All I could do was nod my head and oblige.

Chasiti

I looked at my phone to make sure my mind wasn't playing tricks on me. Yea I was a church girl but I knew when someone sent me to voicemail. Gavon wanted to play games and I wasn't in the mood for kiddie games. I decided to take a shower in order to clear my mind. What I really wanted to do was put some clothes on and go find Gavon and bust his head open but I knew Shenita was not about to let me out of the house.

Whatever Shenita was cooking had my whole house smelling just like New Orleans and the way my stomach was growling I couldn't wait to get a taste. She had her bounce music going and she was in the kitchen getting it. I couldn't help but laugh as she held the butter knife to her lips as she sang along with the music on her iPod.

"Guh come on and busta' move wit cha girl. This song right here make you say forget about a dude," Shenita said grabbing my hand.

I wasn't in much of a mood to dance and I knew she had picked up on it.

"What's wrong with cho?"

"I'm okay it doesn't matter anyway."

"What cho mean it don madda'. If it got cho looking like someone pissed in youn' cereal then I need to know."

Her accent was so thick it took me a minute to understand what she was saying.

"I called to check on Gavon and he sent me to voicemail. So just like I told you earlier cuz, I know he's cheating."

"So ya think he cheating huh? I tell ya what. He got the right chick in town cause' I'll find out. Don't worry your pretty little face. Owww you better hope it ain't

Chardonnay! Cause baybee when I see ha, she gon wish she never woulda crossed that line," Shenita said getting hype and jumping around the kitchen. Under any other circumstance the scene would have been funny but Chasiti just wanted whatever was going on and in her case it was no laughing matter.

"What you cooking," I asked changing the subject. I really wasn't trying to talk about Chardonnay right now.

"I told you earlier mudbugs. And don't worry I'll teach you how to eat them. I'm gone cook Jean'nae something else, she already came in her rolling her eyes at me. I told her she keep on playin' wit me if she want to and watch what happens. Anyway what time does Gee get home?"

"He should be here in another hour or so," I told her over my shoulder. My breasts were starting to hurt so I knew it was time to nurse Lil' Gee again. I had already heard him in his crib stirring when I walked past his nursery a few moments ago. Heading back in that direction and entering his room, I picked him up and positioned my nose under his little neck. He smelt so good and I wished that I could bottle that smell up and keep it forever.

I eased down in the nursing chair in his room with his boppy pillow so I could get comfortable. As I nursed him he looked up at me looking just like his great grandma. If only Mama Jean was here Gavon wouldn't be acting like this. Lil' Gavon gave out a burp that sounded like one his father would let out when he got a good meal causing me to laugh.

Placing him in his car seat I took him back into the kitchen area and sat him next to the table. Shenita was adamant about me eating those nasty crawfish and just like with Mama Jean, I knew not to sass her either.

"See looka here you got to take the tail and twist it a lil bit, and then you pop off like that doh. Nie this where I like to suck the juice out. If you don't get the juice outta tha head of the crawfish cho might as well get up from the table heffa. Don't get prissy on me Chasiti nie. Dat juice is good.

Now after you get the juice out, then you get the tail and pull the first lil ring off and BAM! There go your meat. Now I showed you the prissy way but I'm gon' eat them my way," Shenita schooled me as I sat with my face scrunched up.

After a while Shenita had me rolling in laughter at her and some of the stories she was telling me. I was all good and almost out of my slump, that was until Gavon walked in.

"Wassup? What y'all doing? Oh snap you cooked mudbugs?" He asked getting all hype while rubbing his hands together.

"What cho been doing doh?" Shenita looked at him sucking the juice out of her crawfish and ignoring his question.

"What you mean what I been doing? My wife right here, I don't answer to you cuz," He laughed.

"Yea whateva," Shenita said.

"Let me go change so I can join y'all."

Gavon walked off down the hall and came back a few minutes later dressed in a white tee and basketball shorts. Of course Jean'nae was stuck to his leg. No matter how mad I was at him, there was no denying how fine that man was. Instead of joining in the conversation I continued to eat my crawfish while Shenita gave him the third degree. There was no denying that she had some skills in the kitchen and no matter how I protested these here mudbugs earlier, the fact that I had bitten my fingers four times and my tongue twice let it be known she was right!

Once I had had enough and was good and full, I cleaned myself up before I got the kids ready for bed.

"Wassup you with Chas?" Gavon asked me as he got ready for the shower. I was boiling on the inside because before he left a few hours ago he had taken a shower and here he was again taking another one. He even sat on the other side of the table away from me. Claiming he needed a lot of space so that he could dig in to his food.

"Nothing I'm good. Wassup with you?" I asked him looking up from my tablet. It took everything in me not to call him out but I remained calm. I needed God to tell me when to speak because if I spoke on my own it was not going to be anything Christ like coming out.

"You acting funny that's all. Maybe it's that baby blues stuff everybody been telling me about."

"Hmph," I said before he paused and watched me briefly before he walked in the bathroom and shut the door. Another thing that he did that was out of character for him. I couldn't remember the last time he had closed the door to our bathroom considering it was inside of our bedroom.

Gavon still hadn't said anything about Chardonnay and to me it only made him seem guiltier. He had left his phone on his side of the bed and as bad as I wanted to I

wasn't going to bother looking through it. Papa had always

told me that when you go looking for something don't be

mad when you find it. I knew prayer would bring

everything to the light sooner or later and I hoped that I

would be able to handle it all.

Gavon came out the bathroom with stream coming

off his body and water glistening over his muscles. I turned

my lamp off on my side of the bed and threw the cover

over my body with an attitude. It didn't make any sense

how God made this man so sexy. It wasn't long before I

felt Gavon pulling his side of the covers back but he never

got in the bed. Instead he walked around to my side and

kneeled down right in my face.

"Bae you know I love you right?"

"Mmhhmm," I said.

"I'm glad to have you and the kids in my life. I love

you with everything in me Chas," he said removing the

cover from my face and kissing my lips before he got up to get in the bed.

I wonder why it was so easy for men to lay with another woman and come home to his main chick like nothing ever happened. Gavon eased under me and wrapped his hand around me until his hand was resting in his favorite place under my breast. He knew this position would put both of us to sleep.

No More Thuggin

Gavon

I left Chas in the bed as I tended to the kids. Shenita was in her bed snoring like she hadn't slept in days. Knowing her she'd been partying and bopping every weekend. Jean'nae wanted her waffle warmed up and a scrambled egg with cheese. I never saw a child eat cheese like Jean'nae. She would eat a whole pack of cheese if we let her.

Lil' Gee was just flat out greedy. At four days old he wanted more than four ounces of milk and already he would keep his fist in his mouth. Just as I had kissed him on his cheek and was about to lay him down the doorbell rang. It was only a little after seven so I was wondering who was coming to my house this early. Especially uninvited.

"Wassup son," my Pops walked right in and took Gavon out of my arms. I closed the door behind him.

"Pops you ain't even wash your hands yo."

"My fault. I been working and I missed my grandbabies."

My dad was about his business and I couldn't knock him for that. He had done his time and since he was finally exonerated he was able to get a good paying job which was a blessing. My only problem was him moving on so fast to be with another woman.

"Where my daughter in law?"

"I'm letting her rest. She's been a little on edge lately," I told him.

"What did you do son?"

"Why do I have to be the one to do anything?"

"Well women don't act funny just for no reason. You not tipping are you?"

"Man go head on with that. While we on the subject, you need to fall back out of the faces of all of these random women."

My Pops jaws tightened. He was about to say something when Shenita walked in the kitchen.

"Who dat with all dis fuss goin on doh?" Shenita rubbed her eyes.

"Shenita what's going on niece?"

"Uncle Al wassup doh?" It had been a long time since they had seen one another but one thing about it the two of them didn't miss a beat with one another.

"Your cousin in here with all that rah and I ain't really trying to hear it this early in the morning. I just want to spend some time with my grandbabies before I go home and knock out."

"Well since everyone is here I might as well get breakfast started," Shenita said.

"You don't have to do that Nita. Jean'nae done ate," I stopped her.

"Chasiti ain't ate doh."

"You right," I said.

Shenita and my Pops looked at me funny like I had done something wrong. Instead of staying to hear what it was I turned to walk out of the kitchen and bumped right into Chasiti.

"I'm sorry bae. You okay?"

"I'm good."

I wanted to continue my conversation with my Pops but instead of pressing it in front of everybody I let it go for now. The time would come and when it did he would know just how serious I really was. He can feel how he wanted but I wasn't playing with him about this other woman. I took my phone off the charger and put my passcode in. I knew better than to have a passcode on my phone but I hadn't erased the conversation that Chardonnay and I had out of my phone yet. I was still keeping the secret from Chasiti about her being back in town. Especially now that Chardonnay was pregnant as well.

I looked down at my phone and went into my messages. Something was off about my phone. I had a message from Chardonnay about twenty minutes ago but it was opened and read. I knew Chasiti hadn't been through my phone because I had a complex passcode that she couldn't get through. I went ahead and deleted the messages and stuck my phone in my pocket.

Just as soon as I slid my hand from my pocket Chasiti walked in the room and giving me a knowing look. I wasn't used to this whole postpartum stuff but she needed to come out of it quick because I wasn't feeling it. Instead of saying anything to her I went back to join my Pops and Shenita in the living room.

"So who dis woman that got cho face all in the phone?" I heard Shenita ask my old man as I was making my way back in the living room.

My Pops looked up at me and ran his hand over his face while shaking his head.

"You can answer," I told him.

"Why you got so much hostility in your voice son? You act like it's a crime to date."

"It is a crime to date if you say you love my mama."

Instead of responding back to her he simply got up and gave Lil' Gee to Chasiti who had just entered the kitchen.

"I'll holla at y'all in a few days. Maybe then my son will grow up and understand that I have needs too."

"Whatever man," I waved him off. I brushed pass Chasiti and went in the other room. Sitting in my recliner I turned the TV on to try and drown out everything and everyone around me. My only time to watch TV was before bed but since I had no church business today I was going to be watching Sports Center all day today.

"Gavon," Chasiti came in the room placing my son on his stomach since he was sleep.

"What Chas?" I clearly had an attitude.

"First off you can check the attitude. I think it's time for your dad to move on, it's been years Gavon."

"Here you go. Who side you on Chas? Seriously! You round here rooting for a dude that professes his love for my mom every chance he get but the first piece of tail come by he trying to hop on it. Man go head on."

"So if I die today, you not gone move on?" Chasiti asked me.

It made me look at her like was crazy. She knew what I had to go through to be with her, I was confused on what would even make her think I would be able to move on.

"Nah I ain't moving on," I stated.

"Pssh you already have," she said under her breath.

"What you said?"

"Nothing," she walked out leaving the baby with me.

I heard what she said which lead me to believe she knew about me and Chardonnay. That scared me a little bit because I wanted to know how much she knew.

"Aye cuz you cool? Why you beefin' with Uncle Al? You kno' he need sexual healing too baybee," Shenita stood in the door twirling her big hips.

"Gone Shenita," I laughed at her.

"Nah but fo'real. I want you to spend some time with Chas today. I got enough titty milk to last my lil whoadie for hours and don't worry bout little Ms. Jean'nae cause' I'm gon' have her right fo I leave Gawga."

With everything going on I did need to spend some time with my wife, especially since I felt like she had a clue about Chardonnay. I was feeling guilty so although she was in the other room I grabbed my phone and sent her a text to pop us some popcorn and meet me in the bed so we can watch a movie. Chasiti loved when I did all that lovey dovey girlie stuff with her. If I didn't get back on my A game this could possibly be the end of my marriage and I

knew that it wouldn't be any one's fault but mine.

No More Thuggin

Chardonnay

Kendrick came home from work with his small check and his work boots off throwing them down on the floor. My whole day consisted of cleaning up behind him. He had a problem with making me feel inferior to him and if I didn't know any better I think he liked it that way.

When I first met him he held the word of God to such a high standard but after the second year of marriage things began to fall apart. I was no longer his help meet who walked beside him but more like the help that walked behind him doing as I was told.

"This it Ken?" I waved the check in his face with one hand and rubbing my stomach with the other.

"Chardonnay it was your choice to move back here. I'm not even from here, you are. I took a big pay cut to move to this slow behind town."

I walked over to where he had thrown his boots and picked them up then wobbled towards the closet to put them in their proper place. Kendrick didn't know it but I'd called his job and he hadn't worked but three days this pay period. That's why his check was so small. I came out of the closet and looked over at him with a scowl on my face.

"Ken you can stop blaming me for moving back home. If you would've kept your little man in your pants in the first place then we wouldn't be here now would we? You had women showing up to our house trying to jump on me. So I would like it if you took some responsibility for us having to relocate."

I was livid and the smug look that he had on his face was disgusting me. One thing I could say was when I was with Gavon he wanted to give me the world and if I could go back and change some things, the way I treated him would definitely be one of them. It was like my daughter could understand what I was thinking and at that very moment she kicked. I guess she was missing the calmness of her father just like I was.

"Chardonnay not tonight. I already told you that I changed and I'm not even on that anymore."

"Did you Ken? Because I think you brought the same problem with us."

Kendrick took his shirt off and threw it on the floor followed by his pants and briefs. He walked into the bathroom like he didn't catch what I said when I knew good and well he heard me.

Just like the good wife I was, I went behind him and picked the rest of his clothes up. Instead of complaining to him I walked the clothes to the laundry room so I could wash them first thing in the morning. I was too exhausted to do anything else tonight. Just as I threw his pants on the pile with his other jeans the air in my body got caught in my throat as a gold paper fell out of his pocket.

I knew that this couldn't be what I thought it was. Clearly he couldn't be that stupid to leave evidence on himself once he returned home. I walked back over just to see what it was and sure enough it was a condom wrapper. When I was with Gavon I didn't have to worry about him cheating on me it was the other way around. Maybe this was God's way of making me reap what I had sown.

Heading back to our room I was armed with a black skillet in my right hand along with the Magnum wrapper in my left and waited for Kendrick to get out the shower. The funny thing was that the wrapper said XL but I knew that was a lie from the pits of hell!

Ten minutes later he came out with water beading off his tatted chest. Kendrick was a nice caramel complexion with dark eyes. He kept his hair cut low. His waves in his head would make a blind person sea sick. His beard was long and thick just like I loved it and was the best feature on my husband. I loved every bit of my husband I just hated his dog ways. All he had to do was lick his lips and smile and he would get me every time.

"What's this Ken?" I held the evidence between my pointer and middle finger.

"What you doing with that?" He asked as he dried his face.

"I found it in your pants Ken. The same pants you just took off. It surely ain't mine."

"Nah that ain't mine either. I know you didn't get that out my pants."

I threw the condom at him and walked off. There was no winning with him. He always made me feel like I didn't know what I was talking about even if I had the facts right in his face.

"Chardonnay that's not mine baby. Oh wait you know what? I remember now. One of my co-workers asked me to hold it for him until after work and I forgot to give it back to him."

"You sound stupid Ken."

He tried to grab me but I snatched away and walked out of the room and straight out of the front door. I was glad my car was keyless, too bad I never got to drive it since Kendrick was always gone in it. I pushed the start button and peeled out of the driveway with Kendrick standing in the window staring at me. I wasn't even surprised that he didn't try and come behind me to make me come back. I he didn't care that I only had on one of his shirts and a pair of his boxers.

As soon as I got to the first stop light I pulled out my phone to text Gavon. I needed to see him but I knew it was going to be hard to get him out the house this time of the night. I knew that he had a new baby at home and a wife as well but he was the only one who I could trust and could help me to feel better.

Me: Can you meet me real quick?

Von: Do you see the time? It's almost midnight. What am I supposed to tell Chas?

Me: Come up with something. I need you right now.

Von: Text me the spot.

I texted Gavon the location to where I was and waited. I loved Kendrick more than anything but why couldn't he be more like Gavon. For me to find a condom wrapper in Kendrick's pocket let me know that he really wasn't trying to get caught this time. And I say that because he had given me so many STD's in the last year and a half it wasn't funny.

We had to flee from South Carolina because I couldn't go out in public without a woman trying to jump on me about my husband. The man that I married!

I tried to calm myself down while I waited on Gavon. I pulled out my phone and since I knew it may take him some time to get away I downloaded a few games and scrolled through Instagram to see if Chasiti had posted any pictures of their new baby.

Gavon's all black F-150 pulled up, I unlocked the doors and cleared my history on my phone. I didn't want to show the excitement on face when the door popped open so I continued to look down on my phone. My car filled up with Bath and Body Works causing me to look up from my phone and into the face of Chasiti as she sat in the passenger seat with a scowl on her face.

"Wasn't expecting to see me were you?" Chasiti said with an attitude.

"Chas let me explain," I told her.

"Heifer only my friends call me Chas and I don't consider you a friend. Now why are you texting my husband? Better yet where is *your* husband since you got that big rock on your finger."

"Chasiti there is no need for the name calling. You can get out of my car with all the disrespect. I've been nothing but respectful to you."

"Have you Chardonnay? You've been occupying a lot of my husband's time, behind my back might I add, and you want to talk to me about *disrespect*? This is a fair warning to you, stay away from my husband."

"Please boo boo just remember how you got him is how you can lose him. Get your big behind out of my car," I told Chasiti.

She planted her manicured finger on my forehead, "You better be lucky you pregnant. I'll be big but please don't get it twisted. Just know this is *exactly* how Gavon likes it. Only a dog wants a bone," she finished before getting out and slamming my door.

The last thing Chasiti wanted was to start with me. I was the right chick to break up her little happy home. She mugged me one last time before pulling off in Gavon's

truck while I sat there envying her.

Chasiti

"Guh where you been? You kno' you not supposed to be out the house yet," Shenita said as soon as I walked back in the house. I was so mad that I knew she could see the smoke coming from my ears.

"I know that but when Chardonnay texted Gee's phone I had to go see about that heffa."

Shenita grabbed her chest and made a strange face, "Heffa I kno' you ain't left outta dis house and left without me. You got some balls First Lady," Shenita busted out laughing.

"Don't let the church in me fool you Nita. I'm sick of her."

"I told you let me get a hold of ha."

"She's pregnant so we got to chill."

"No she betta chill," Shenita said with an attitude.

I was too wound up but I knew that if I didn't get my behind back in the bed and Gavon woke up it was going to be a mess. I wouldn't be able to look at him in his face feeling the way that I was because I would have jumped on him this here night.

"Night Nita."

"Night girl. Get you some rest and don't worry about the babies. I got them."

"Thanks girl."

I walked in my bedroom where Gavon was laying there sleeping peacefully. I eased into the cover up under him.

"Where you been?" he rolled over.

God you better take him back to sleep right now before I do it. I thought to myself.

"Nowhere," I lied.

He raised his head up from the pillow, "You lying now?"

"I went to get some fresh air."

"You know it ain't safe out there. And this late? Just let me know next time you get ready to leave out the house."

"Alright," I said closing my eyes. Gavon wrapped his hands around me and got into our normal position. I wanted so bad for him to take his hands off of me but I had to play it off.

Sleep was not finding me easily so I decided to go check on Lil' Gavon. He was sleeping looking like a little angel so I went to get something to drink. Shenita was still up in the living room caking with some dude on the phone. I popped her on her big leg and shook my head at her. She stuck her tongue out at me like Cardi B does on Love and Hip Hop. Shenita was a mess but it was calming to have her here with us.

I was starting to feel bad about how I acted earlier with Chardonnay. Well for calling her names. I went with the intentions of getting the information out of her that she had been holding but the sight of her made me sick. I wanted to know what she wanted with my husband when she had her own man at home. I walked around the house for a while because my spirit was so unsettled and as soon as I went back in our bedroom Gavon was up and sitting on the side of the bed with the light on.

"Is it something you want to talk about Chas?" he asked with his back to me.

"No," I said and took a sip of my water.

"I mean you walking around the house with beef. You sneaking out the house and stuff. What's going on with you?" he walked towards me.

"I'm good Gee okay."

"I'm saying though we can talk about it if something is bothering you. Just let me know."

"I'm good," I said placing my cup on the side of my bed and getting under the cover. I knew this conversation wasn't over but I was done for tonight. I was still sore from my C-Section and I needed to rest. Gavon stood there a few more minutes before he got back in the bed.

Gavon tossed and turned all night in his sleep. I could tell something was bothering him. While he was questioning me I should've been asking him what was on his mind. I think him asking me questions was a way to throw me off his trail, but I was hot on it. And if I ever caught him it was going to be hell to pay. My head started pounding just thinking about it. I hadn't realized how late it was until I saw the sun was starting to come up so I allowed the pain meds I had taken to consume me as I drifted off to sleep.

No More Thuggin

Gavon

It was only a little after seven in the morning when I decided to head to the church. I needed some one on one time with God because things were beginning to spiral out of control. Had I not been in my feelings about what my Pops was doing I would have gone to him as well but I just couldn't get the thought of him moving on out of my head. I knew that my mother would probably be turning over in her grave if she knew how he was carrying on.

After showering and getting dressed in my comfortable attire, jeans, J's, and v-neck tee. I knew that when I went out to do ministry I had to make sure the people received me in order to get the message that I had for them from God. If I had constantly worn a suit and tie or my preaching robe I knew that would only turn them away. And in all honesty this was where I was the most comfortable. Because I came from the streets I felt like God was sending me back into those same streets to help bring them out. Who better to relate to them than someone they saw as one of them?

I found my snapback and tied up my dreads before placing a kiss on my wife's cheek. When she didn't move I knew that she was in a deep sleep and would be out for a while. She needed the rest though because she had been going since she got home from the hospital.

Making sure my little man and princess were both changed and fed, I took the baby monitor to the living room where I heard my big mouth cousin yapping away on the phone.

"You still on that phone Nita?"

"You still in my business Gavon?" she asked me with a slight attitude.

I took a step back and looked at her trying to figure out where that had come from. Shenita and I were always close and I couldn't remember not one time that she and I had fallen out. Even as kids we had gotten along so for her to be acting funny right now threw me for a loop.

"Let me call you back bae. What? Boy naw. Gavon know not to try me. I be thuggin!" she laughed.

Just as fast as she had gotten mad the dude on the other end must have made changed his tone and was making her feel better. A huge smile began to form on her face as she took her finger and twirled a piece of hair round it.

"Yes baybee I love you too. What? Boy stop you know you can't talk to me like that while I'm in this here house. Gavon may tell Jesus on us. I'm trying to make it in one day and I don't need no glitch in the system. I'll call you back," Shenita said as she ended the call.

She was a trip but I loved her no matter what. Before I could let her know what I was about to do she spoke first.

"You gone make me and Chas cut you."

"Wait…what…why?"

"Cause you stupid that's why. You got a brand new baby, a three year old daughter, and a hormonal wife that need you but you out here sneakin' and geekin' in the next broad's face," she spat.

I didn't know what on earth she was talking about. Could Chasiti know what was going on with Chardonnay and I? Had I not been covering my tracks like I should?

"Don't stand there now all quiet and answer me."

"I have no idea what you're talking about cuz. You know how I feel about my wife. I would never do anything to intentionally hurt her or my family."

"That's what cho mouf say but let me put you up on game real quick. Let me find out you doing anything behind her back and it's going to be me and you. That woman loves you and the funky draws you take off at night, so if you hurt her I'm coming fo' dat lil beady head you got." And with that she walked out of the room snatching the baby monitor from my hand and entering her room.

I didn't know how much my cousin or wife knew or if they were just fishing for information because they had no real info. Either way I had to make this right. There were already too many Pastors in the pulpit who had scandals attached to their names where other women were involved and I was not trying to be the next.

***

The closer I got to the church that I was now pastoring the more I felt like something was about to go wrong. I didn't know what it was but it was so unsettling and I was beginning to get nervous. Never had I felt like this on the way to the house of God. Even when I was doing my dirt back in the day and accompanying Mama Jean to church I didn't get this feeling.

Mama Jean. Just the thought of her made me wish she was still here. She would know what to tell me or how to help me make sense of everything. As a matter of fact if she was still here I had no doubt that I wouldn't be going through this because she would have made sure I had no dealings with Chardonnay. Besides it was her who was responsible for my grandmother to get so worked up that day and go into cardiac arrest. Even with that knowledge here I was sneaking behind my wife's back for the same woman who caused me hell. But there was just something about her that made me feel like I had to be there, even if it was for a short while.

Pulling into the parking lot I saw that only my assistant Kareem was there. He was always there on time and never complained about the tasks that I needed him to complete for me. I met him one day when I was out doing some street ministry and I came up on him being in an altercation with some dudes. They were beating him so bad until I ran up on them and when they noticed who I was they backed off.

Something about him selling their product on the streets and passing it off as his own. Because they knew me and knew who my uncles were, they decided to let him live. He was barely hanging on by a thread once we made it to the hospital but I didn't leave him. I didn't know of any family to call for him so I felt compelled to be there for him if and when he woke up.

Once he was in his room and had made it out of surgery all I could do way pray for him. It wasn't until I heard him speak that I knew he had heard everything that I had been speaking over his life. I half way thought he was going to be upset and not want to hear about *'my God'* like so many people refer to Him as when I try to minister to them.

"How can I be saved?" His voice was raspy and I knew that it was from the tube that the doctor had taken out of his throat a few hours ago.

"All you have to do is confess your sins and ask Jesus to come into your heart and be your personal savior."

"That's it?"

"That's it," I told him.

I made my way over to pray for him as he followed the instructions I had given to him.

"I don't feel anything. Did I do it right?"

I couldn't help but chuckle because I had encountered so many people who thought being saved was about a feeling instead of understanding that what they had just confessed was more than enough. Once I explained as much as I could to him before sleep took him over I was glad to know that another soul had been won for the Kingdom.

When Kareem got out of the hospital he showed up to the church and asked me to be his mentor. After a few months of him sitting under me I discussed with Chasiti how she would feel to have him as our assistant. She was in agreement because she knew that God had done a new thing in Kareem and this was just what he needed to stay on the straight and narrow. From that day forward he had been with us and I thanked God for his life.

"Morning Pastor. You're here early," Kareem said looking up from behind his computer.

He had done a complete 180 and looked nothing like his old self. Don't get me wrong he still had swag about himself the way he dressed some days but his appearance in the spirit was what I was referring to. The glory of God was shining bright on him.

"Yea I needed to come in and spend some time talking to God. There is so much going on that I need some clear instructions on how to handle it all," I told him.

Instead of responding he just nodded his head in understanding. Before I could turn and walk down the hallway towards the sanctuary he stopped me.

"Oh I almost forgot. Mrs. Andrews said she would be here to see you at ten. I told her you weren't expected to be in today but she said that there was no doubt that you would be in after last night," he said looking at me funny.

I was just as confused as he was as to what Chardonnay was talking about. How did she figure that I would be in and what had happened last night to make her think that?

"I know this may not be my place," Kareem started, "But you have always been real with me since I met you and it's only right that I return it. Now I don't know what is really going on nor do I want to but I don't think it's a good idea to meet with a woman and First Lady not be here. The last thing you need is a church scandal on your hands," he finished.

This was confirmation for me from God. Like He was telling me once again through someone else that a scandal could possibly happen. Considering I had the same thoughts on my way over here.

"I hear you Kareem and I appreciate you for looking out for me. But trust me this meeting won't be behind closed doors and I'm sure it will be quick.

Surrendering and waving his white flag, Kareem said no more before going back to the task he was completing. I appreciated him looking out for me and I knew that he only had my best interest at heart. I hated to admit it but he was right about Chasiti needing to be there when I met up with Chardonnay but it was too late. I was already in way over my head and this was why I needed to fall on my face at the altar and talk with God.

The scripture that keeps coming back to my remembrance is the one in Romans chapter seven and verse fifteen.

'I don't really understand myself, for I want to do what is right, but I don't do it. Instead I do what I hate.'

That was exactly what I felt like each time I met up with Chardonnay. I didn't want to go behind my wife's back but here I was doing it. I knew it wasn't right but the tugging at my heart kept me going back. I just prayed that in the end everything would be worked out.

"Gavon!" I heard coming from behind me as soon as I had opened the door to the sanctuary. I already knew who it was without turning around but I did anyway.

Not bothering to open my mouth I could tell just by the look on Chardonnay's face this was not about to be one of our normal meeting sessions.

"This is the first and last time I'm going to say this. Tell Chasiti if she comes at me one more time like she did last night I won't care if I'm pregnant or not. I'm beating that behind!"

Hold on. What did she mean 'like Chasiti did last night'? I guess my face wore the same confused look that my mind felt because she answered causing my world to stop.

"That's right when I needed you last night after Kendrick and I got into it guess who showed up after I text you my location? That's right your precious wife Chasiti."

Jesus take me now.

No More Thuggin

Alvin

I knew that once Gavon found out I was interested in someone he would be a little upset but never did I think it would be this bad. It was like every time I saw him now he looked at me with such hatred and confusion in his eyes and that bothered me.

In the beginning when I got out of jail we had begun to rebuild our relationship as father and son. I did my best to explain to him everything that happened to his mother and expressed to him how much I loved the both of them. It killed me to see how he broke down but I was trusting in God to give him comfort, and for a while He had. Now that I was moving on it was like he was hurting all over again. The last thing I wanted to do was cause him any more pain but I needed to live my life too.

I did my best to understand where he was coming from and how he was feeling. It was hard for him to not remember his mother and hate me for what he thought I did to her. I figured he felt like I shouldn't be able to move on so fast but in all actuality it wasn't that at all. It had been almost thirty years and now that I had another chance at living again, I didn't want to continue to live my life by myself.

I finished getting myself ready for my day once I got some much needed rest. Thank God I was off for the next two days so that I could relax. I had planned on stopping by the church on my way to lunch with Marisa. I needed to talk to my son to see if we could get pass what we were going through. I wanted nothing more than to get him on board with this relationship I was in because my feelings for Marisa were getting stronger by the day.

Getting out of the shower I brushed my teeth and brushed my hair down making sure not to go against the wave pattern in my head. Looking at myself I could see how the many years of working out behind bars had definitely done my body some good. I knew I was a lady magnet but I was also the last of a dying breed when it came to being a faithful man. If I committed myself to someone I was going to make sure that she never felt second to anyone but God.

I took one last look at my chiseled caramel chest and handsome face and made my way to my room to get dressed. I decided on wearing some khaki pants with a blue and green plaid shirt with some navy blue loafers. Placing my watch on my arm and one gold cross chain around my neck, I was ready as soon as I sprayed a little Givenchy Pi on myself. Marisa had gotten it for me a few weeks back just because she loved the way it smelled.

Making sure to lock the house up I got in my car just as my phone rang. Smiling at the sight of Marisa's face popping up on my screen I answered it with a smile evident in my voice.

"Hey baby," I said backing out of the driveway. I was so blessed to be able to come home and not have to worry about a place to live because between Gavon and his uncles Reno and Danny, they made sure that the house Mama Jean lived in was now mine free and clear. That was a life saver and allowed me to be able to save and even put something aside for my grandbabies.

"We still on for lunch?"

Her voice was as smooth as silk and I could listen to it forever.

"You already know beautiful. I'm just going to swing by the church and see my son before I head over to you," I said.

"Don't worry baby. He will come around soon enough," Marisa said noticing the change in my voice.

"I can totally understand what he is feeling because I felt the same way about my mother after my father passed. I didn't understand right away and the more I complained she eventually left her boyfriend alone. The change I saw in her because she was lonely is what made me see things from her point of view."

"Wow I didn't know that. I pray that things don't come to that with us because I don't plan on letting you go for anything," I told her honestly.

"And I don't plan on you letting me go either," she blushed.

"Well let me get in here real quick and I'll text you when I'm headed your way."

"Ok baby. Be careful and I love you," she said shocking the both of us. It wasn't because she said it first that threw me it was because it was at that exact moment I knew I felt the same way and it was mind blowing.

I had been thinking I was falling in love with Marisa but I kept talking myself out of the feeling thinking that maybe I was moving too fast. The last thing I wanted to do was push her away because she wasn't on the same page with me about her feelings, but now I knew that I had to get my son on board with this because it was now real.

"I love you too baby," I told her before ending the call.

I sat in the parking lot of the church for a few minutes grinning like a Chester cat at the thought of finally being able to experience love again. I knew that this would be what my late wife wanted and finally I was at peace in that area.

I got out of the car and made my way inside to be greeted by Gavon's assistant Kareem who let me know where Gavon was. It was so good to see the impact that my son was making in the lives of people and it made me proud to see him walking and operating in his calling. I knew that both his mother and grandmother were smiling down on him from heaven.

Just as I had walked into the sanctuary I saw the lights were dim and heard voices coming from the back leading into the kitchen that was back there. I was just

about to open the door when I heard a woman ask,

"Gavon what are we going to do about this baby?"

Chardonnay

Gavon had a look of stress on his face after I asked him about the baby. I didn't want to keep stressing him but I was in between a rock and a hard place. I needed his input on what to do. Kendrick was too busy doing him so there was no talking to him about anything.

"Uhmm."

Someone behind us cleared their throat and caused both of us to turn around nervously. Seeing Alvin in the door with his arms folded across his chest made me look at Gavon. Gavon was looking uneasy.

"What's up Pops," Gavon got up and walked towards his dad.

"Nothing. What's up with you?" Alvin looked around Gavon to look at me. I shot him a cute innocent smile.

I pranced my pregnant self right on over to Alvin because we hadn't officially met yet and I always wanted to meet Gavon's dad. Looking at him I saw where Gavon got his good looks from. Alvin didn't look like he spent any time in prison.

"How are you? I'm Chardonnay," I smiled at him and held my hand out.

"Hi Chardonnay," he replied dryly but never returned the gesture. I put my hand down and looked up at Gavon.

"Chardonnay I'll talk to you later," Gavon tried rushing me off.

"But you never answered my question," I said to Gavon.

"Chardonnay that's something you got to figure out not me."

"Oh really," I placed my hands on my hip. "Alright. Just remember what I said about your wife."

The look Alvin gave Gavon let me know that I was going to be the topic of their conversation. I really didn't care, if Gavon was going to ride with me on this then his opinion mattered as well. I made it to my car and dreaded going home to Kendrick. He was off today and I knew that he would be laying around the house all day playing his game.

When I arrived home the smell of food instantly hit my nose which was something new. Walking further into the house I noticed that Kendrick had even picked up his stuff that he had left on the floor when I went to go and meet Gavon. I entered the kitchen to see my husband with the phone to his ear while he stood over the stove stirring something in a pot. I stood there silently to see if I could figure out who it was that he was talking to. We hadn't been back in Savannah very long so I wanted to know what chick had him wanting to cheat on his wife. All these females in Savannah knew not to play with me. I didn't mind getting down with anybody. Pregnant and all I will pullup on any broad. I got mad just standing there thinking about someone from Savannah trying me.

"Yea well let me finish cooking this meal for her and I'll see you tonight. Make sure you do that there for me now," Kendrick said and licked his lips.

"Do what Kendrick?" I slapped him in the back of his head causing him to drop his phone. I knew when it fell it was cracked.

"Chardonnay come on man I was talking to my mama," he explained.

"Oh. Now. You. Want. To. Lie," I said punching him after every word. All he could was ball up. I punched him one last time before I walked to our bedroom. I tried slamming the door in his face but he blocked it and busted in on me.

"Aye man why you acting like that? How you know I wasn't talking to my mama?"

"Ain't nobody stupid Ken. Your mama don't even stay here. You just told that chick you will see her tonight. But I doubt you will be going anywhere tonight buddy."

"Okay," he said rubbing his hand down his beard. "What dude you been spending all your time with? Since we going in on these questions."

"What you talking bout'?" I looked confused.

"Now you want to act like you don't know. See the other day when I left here, I know you had another dude in my house. I don't wear Gucci cologne."

I was speechless. I thought I covered all of my tracks. I could kick myself in the butt for this slip up. Kendrick had no real evidence except the cologne and I could lie about that.

"I'm not the one cheating here Kendrick you are. Don't try to use that reverse psychology on me," I told him with a straight face.

"Chardonnay if I find out you got a dude in my house it's over with for you and him. I don't play games like that. Play around with me if you want to Chardonnay because you know how I get down. Now I sit around here and let you hit and slap on me but you will not bring me away from my comfort zone only to be laid up with the next dude. Since the floor is open is that baby you carrying even mine?"

I slapped Kendrick across his caramel colored face so hard as the crocodile tears flowed. I had to put on a show for him since he was like a hound. I knew Gavon could not step foot back in this house and I hated it. He brought so much comfort and a sense of calm when he came to the house and that's what I needed to feel. It was because of Gavon that I was still able to look Kendrick in the face.

"Chardonnay I done told you about your hands. This my last time saying it. I've never hit you and I would like that same respect," Kendrick said.

"Whatever dog!" He had some nerve complaining about me bruising his face up when he was constantly bruising my heart.

Instead of continuing to argue with me Kendrick headed back to our room, changed clothes and walked back out the door. I didn't know where he was going and I was nervous. I grabbed my phone to call Gavon and hoped that he hadn't already gotten started with church. When I got his voicemail, my assumptions were right. We only had one car so I couldn't go anywhere.

I stomped into my bedroom and flopped on the bed. If I didn't calm down I wouldn't be carrying this baby full term. This baby was my only hope to keep the man I loved. Feeling defeated all I could do was lay across the bed and cry. If changing my life for the better was this hard I was about to revert back to my old selfish self. And everybody knew exactly how Char got down.

No More Thuggin

Gavon

After arguing with my Pops about what he thought he heard. He was finally leaving. I was sweating bullets talking to him. I don't know why Chardonnay wanted to pop up at the church of all places to talk. This was the worse place she could possibly come to.

I did the best that I could to prepare for service like I usually did but it was hard. Trying to get up to teach and bring a word from God with everything I had going on in my life was far from being easy. I needed God to decrease me and increase Himself.

As I was teaching today I noticed a young man in the back that had a look of stress all over his face. Something was pulling me towards him all during service and I needed to make sure to speak to him before he had the chance to leave. I talked to a few of the members before I was able to finally head towards him.

He wore a nice flannel shirt, a pair of nice ripped jeans and a hard pair of Yeezy's. I was a sneaker head so I wasn't afraid to compliment another man on his shoes. I approached him just as he was walking out the door.

"Nice shoes man," I told him.

"Preciate that man," he said looking down at his phone.

"I'm the Pastor here. It's not your average church but the presence of God is here," I held my hand out for him to shake it.

"I'm Kendrick," he took my hand. I swallowed real hard once he introduced himself. I hadn't seen any pictures of Kendrick around their house so I never knew what he looked like. He looked nothing like Chardonnay said. She made him out to be a real street dude but he appeared to look like a nerd besides the long beard he had on his face. The Malcolm X glasses made me think he had a PhD.

"Well what brings you here Kendrick? I'm Gavon but everybody calls me Gee," I played it off as we walked towards one of the tables in the room.

The inner part of the sanctuary didn't look like the ordinary church that held row after row of pews along with a pulpit. God gave me a vision to make it different. Being that I was from the streets I understood that mentality so if I wanted to bring those young men and women in I had to have a place they would feel comfortable in.

Most churches that were set up the traditional way could turn people off because they felt out of place. They would feel like the people as well as the pastor were unapproachable and I needed to change that. Having the inside somewhat feel like a club with the stage being my pulpit made it relatable and easy to get into the word. I mean if we could turn up in a club when we were out in the world why couldn't we put that same energy into praising God.

"Just marriage problems. Your message today really hit close to home you feel me. My wife pregnant and I believe she's seeing another dude."

"What makes you think that," I asked grabbing both of us a bottle of water.

"I'm a man I know her focus ain't on me. I'm saying bruh, yea, I've done some things myself that I shouldn't have but I'm trying to get it right. I told her from the beginning that I wasn't a one woman man. She wanted me anyway. I'm really trying to work on this thing but my dad raised me to be this way."

I shook my head. I knew all about Kendrick's dog ways but Chardonnay loved him and decided to marry him anyway so there was nothing she could do but stick it out or leave.

"Well I don't think she's doing anything wrong. You said she was pregnant and she may just be emotional. My wife just had a baby last week and she's still going through the emotions. We as men got to step up and play our role so another man won't have a chance to take our place," I looked at him.

"Yea I feel ya. I appreciate you for talking to me."

"Anytime bruh. I love what I do. Take my number down so we can chop it up. You can call me when you feel like you have no else," I told him.

"Yea cause I'm from the Carolina's so this is all new to me. Do you mind me asking what kind of cologne you wearing? I was thinking of going to try something new that my wife may like," Kendrick said.

"My wife usually buys my cologne. I think I put Gucci on this morning I'm not sure."

"Ok cool. I'm about to go check that out. I'll holla at you Gavon," he said standing to his feet and dapped me up.

It was something in his dap that confirmed something was up. He was a cool dude though or maybe I was just on high alert because I needed to go and talk to Chasiti about approaching Chardonnay.

After making sure everything was good at the church and all of the members who needed me were gone I got in my truck and headed home. I was still trying to figure out how to approach the situation because I knew that it was an ugly one.

I pulled up to the house and Shenita had Jean'nae outside wetting her with the water hose. Shenita had only been here a few days and I could already see Jean'nae was changing in a good way. It was my fault my daughter was a brat and got away with so much. Chasiti couldn't stand it so I knew she was enjoying Shenita getting Jean'nae right.

"Let me hold it," I told Shenita. She handed me the water hose and I wet her.

"I know you lyin'! Gee I swea' to gawd if you would've wet my hair I was gon' bust your head wide open. Why would you do dat doe?"

"Man calm your geechee talking self down," I laughed at her.

"Hee my behind," she said before wetting my Jordan's.

"Seriously Nita!" I chased behind her. Everybody knew I didn't play about my shoes. All that weed smoking I did back in the day had me winded so I gave up chasing her. It felt like my lungs were about to come through my chest. Getting myself together I went into the house to cool off.

"What in the world is wrong with you?" Chasiti asked.

"Your crazy behind cousin in law wet my Jordan's man. I just got these last week," I said taking them off by the door.

"Put them outside so they can dry Gavon," she said as she stood in the kitchen rocking my son.

"Did you go and see Chardonnay?" Before I realized it it slipped out of my mouth. She shifted her weight on her other leg and bit her lip. I knew at that moment that I had messed up and because I was heated with Shenita, I spoke when it wasn't time.

"I know good and well you don't call yourself checking be about some female. Especially Chardonnay. You definitely just tried it to capacity but since you care so much about what I do, yea I did go and see her. I gave her fair warning while I was there and now I see it's time for me to give you yours," she said walking up on me. "If you continue to have contact with her. I'm taking my babies and I'm leaving you. I will not be with a man that refuses to respect the vows of our marriage. Why are you in contact with her anyway? Maybe if my ex was still alive I would call him and chill with him and see how you would like that. Now you can play with me if you want to. Come checking me bout another female. While yall sneaking around you might want to sneak over to the beauty supply store and buy her some edges. All these years and she still can't grow any," she said walking away still fussing.

I was so frustrated right now that her little joke about Chardonnay's edges wasn't even funny. I should've calmed down before even speaking about the Chardonnay issue but I put my foot in my mouth. I threw my shoes out the door and went to find Chasiti.

"Chasiti I wish you would talk out the side of your neck about your ex dude. I didn't kill em' so it don't matter."

"Gavon go head on now before this turns ugly. I should go see her again but this time walk the dog on her since she want to run to you telling everything."

"I'm sorry baby. It wasn't like that. I was just asking," I said trying to diffuse the situation. It was my fault that everything was crazy right now and I knew she was only talking to me out of hurt and anger.

"Gavon get out my face. I can't deal with you right now. You better get your act together real fast. You know when you got with me that I didn't play games. Now that I'm a mother all that playing games is out the window for real. Please don't let my fat, pretty face fool you. Now what do you want for dinner?" She stood there staring at me.

No matter how mad she was, she still fulfilled her role as my wife. That's why I had to lay it all on the table with Chasiti but now wasn't the time. I'd already put myself in the doghouse I didn't want to make it worse. I shot her my sexy smile and slapped her on her butt.

"I would like to have you but I still got a few weeks."

She rolled her eyes and walked off. I don't care what size Chasiti was, she was so fine to me. She was confident with it and I loved it. I changed my clothes so I could go back outside with Jean'nae and spend some time with her. I usually was gone all day on Sunday but I was tired and being around my family kept me sane. Hopefully I wouldn't be getting calls from Chardonnay. She caused enough trouble today showing up at the church.

No More Thuggin

Kendrick

I sat in the parking lot of the mall in deep thought. Chardonnay was open with me about her past and I knew Gavon was part of it. He surely didn't fit the description she gave me though. She said he was a lil jit that thought he was bout that life and wasn't but to me Gavon looked like a real thug with his dreads and the way he dressed.

Char told me he sold drugs back in the day so when she wasn't feeling him anymore and he couldn't take what he wanted from her he tried to kill her. He sounded like he was insecure to me but hey that's him.

I wasn't sure what led me to the club he called a church but I couldn't front the boy could definitely preach. He knew who I was just like I knew him. I could tell by the lump that was in his throat when I said my name. I was waiting for him to come clean and let me know he was dealing with my wife again but he never did. I can't respect a man that can't man up. His cologne smelt just like the scent that was lingering around my house.

A short little cutie passed my car as I was sitting there waddling in my problems. I grabbed my phone and ran behind her.

"Hey excuse me. I couldn't help but notice you when you walked by my car. Can I get your name and number? Maybe take you out sometime," I licked my lips.

Lil mama was on point. She had her hair down to her butt, her nails were done and her feet were pretty. That's all that mattered to me. If her feet were jacked up she wouldn't even get a simple conversation from me. Once she flashed me a winning smile I knew I had her. The best thing about not being from here was the girls were gullible to an out of town dude like myself.

I placed my phone in her hand so that she could store her info in it. I had to go spend money on a new phone due to Chardonnay making me crack my other one.

As she put her number in my phone I heard an accent coming from behind me.

I turned around to see who it was coming from because she was super loud but her accent was turning me on. It was the Nawlins' drawl. She was tall and big boned. She was talking on the phone to somebody and her bottom golds were glistening in the sun.

"Here's your phone back," the lil chick said. I took it from her without even looking at her. She didn't know my name and after seeing this stallion before me it no longer mattered.

I waited for the New Orleans chick to walk in the mall before I followed behind her. She went into Victoria's Secret so I followed her. She was so into her conversation that she didn't even know I was following her. After a little while she paid for her stuff and went into the next store.

"Hold on baybee," she said into the phone. "May I help you?" She said to me.

"I was trying to see if I could holla at you real quick."

"Ewww no! You got a wedding ring on doe. I know you lyin'.

I looked at my finger and realized I had on my wedding band. Most women didn't care about a ring, it actually gave them a challenge. She was different I saw. When I looked up from my wedding ring she was back on the phone walking off swing her hair. I needed to go home to my wife because that could've been ugly. I slept with these girls like my wife wasn't from here. I didn't have a chance of getting caught because Chardonnay rarely left the house. Her past wouldn't allow her to.

Getting what I came to get I left back out of the mall and got in my car. I bobbed my head to Plies as I pulled into the interstate to head home. My mind drifted to my life and I thought about how it was hard to let go of the streets. I worked a normal job for the sake of Chardonnay but it was easier to get out in the streets and make that money the way I knew how.

My wife didn't know that I was skipping work most days because I was out in the streets trying to make some real money. Yea I had two girls I fooled with but it was nowhere near as bad as Chardonnay thought.

Pulling into our driveway I decided to park in the garage since I hadn't planned on going out any more today. I cut the car off and headed in the house. Nothing was on but the TV in the living room. I knew with her being pregnant that she would be asleep. Imagine my surprise when I walked into our room to see Chardonnay lying in bed on her phone.

"Who you texting?" I asked and she dropped her phone and tried to play sleep. I walked up to the bed and tried to snatch the phone. She rolled over so fast you wouldn't know she was even pregnant.

"Get off your stomach before you crush my baby, give me the phone Chardonnay."

"Stop Kendrick. Why do you want my phone so bad? I don't go through your phone and I know you got plenty of females listed in yours," Chardonnay said.

She did have a valid point but I would never let her know that. As a matter of fact I'd just gotten a new number today. Even though shorty gave me her number I really wasn't checking for her like I was that New Orleans chick. I had to have her because she was aggressive and I liked that. That was how I ended up with Chardonnay.

"Mmm hmm that's what I thought! You ain't got nothing to say about that do you," Chardonnay said.

We were in the middle of an argument and here I was thinking about other women. I realized that I needed some real help if I was going to get right and make this marriage work.

"Man I ain't trying to hear all that. Give me your phone. I'm trying not to peter-roll your pregnant behind but you pushing it. I can come get the phone, I'm just trying to give you an opportunity to come clean," I told her.

"Come clean for what? You been dirty this whole relationship bruh."

"Char you knew what I was before you pursued me. I told you from the jump I was a dog and I was working on it. You said you was cool with it. What man wouldn't want a woman that's cool with his doggish ways?"

"I was cool with it when we were just dating Ken. Not when we got married dummy."

I rubbed my hand over my face because she was trying her best to avoid giving me her phone and I was getting frustrated. I had just the idea to get this thing turned around in my favor.

"Okay," I reached in my pocket and took my phone out. "Here," I threw the phone at her.

She looked at me like I was crazy and had six eyes or something. Before she could get her thoughts together I walked up to the bed and snatched her phone from her.

"Go through mine. You already know what it is with me. But you on the other hand real sneaky. Oh word? And you got a code on the phone," I chuckled trying to calm myself down.

"You got a code too Ken so don't try me," Chardonnay said.

"It's your birthday man," I shot at her. She gave me another dumb look as she placed the code in my phone.

"What's your code Char?"

She looked up from the phone and gave me six numbers to punch into her iPhone 6s. I wasn't sure what date this was but I was going to find out. As soon as the phone popped open her text thread with a person named *'Von'* popped up. I scrolled back up to the beginning of the thread and began reading. I knew it was Gavon because he was telling her about us meeting up.

I threw her phone against the wall causing damage to both the wall and her phone.

"You had him in my house Chardonnay? You flaw ma. I've never disrespected you openly like this. But you bring this cat up in my house like its sweet?"

"It's nothing like you think Ken I promise," she tried to clean it up and explain herself. Now that her secret was out in the open she wanted to talk things out.

The doorbell went off and we both stood there trying to figure out who was at our door. No one knew we lived here. I never brought any of my chicks over and made sure that I never had anyone of them following me. It rung again and we both headed towards the door. I opened it before looking to see who it was.

"Aye Char you didn't text me back," Gavon said.

No More Thuggin

Chasiti

Gavon thought he was nickel slick but I had his penny change as Mama Jean would say. I never really knew what that meant but it seemed to fit the occasion. I was riding shot gun to Shenita driving in the direction that Gavon thought I didn't know about. The night I saw Chardonnay she thought once I got out of her car and drove off that I was heading home. Had she been on her A game then she would have known I followed her right to her front door. Instead of coming right up on the house I watched from a distance. All I needed was to see where she lived because I knew this piece of information would eventually come in handy.

"I know one thing Gavon better not be over here with the yamp and I better not see ha. I should have been snatched her baybee for killing my Mama Jean. And you should have just let me handle this while you stayed home," Shenita fussed.

I knew she meant well and she could have very well handled this for me but I needed to see this myself. If my husband was once again back in Chardonnay's life he could rest assured that it was a wrap for us. You only got one time to step out on me and I'm done. I don't care what the church folks would think but it was whatever. The love I had for myself wouldn't allow me to be played.

"Nope cause I needed to look the both of them in their eyes and say what I have to say. Turn right here."

"Ohhh you no good sum-," Shenita started as we both locked eyes on the same thing.

Gavon was so into whatever he was doing on his phone that he didn't notice we were following him. He couldn't wait until I was busy making dinner when he told me he would be right back. He claimed he was running to the store and before I could reply he was making his way

out the front door.

Just as fast as I could pick up the phone I called our

next door neighbor Ms. Alma and asked if she would mind

watching the kids for me for a few minutes. As soon as she

walked up on the steps Shenita and I were coming out on to

the porch.

I wasn't too worried about losing him in traffic

because I knew exactly where he was headed. My spirit

was telling me to calm down but I didn't want to hear that

right now. I knew I was being disobedient at that moment

but I didn't care. Everything I had worked so hard for was

in jeopardy and I had to know if this was the end of my

marriage.

We watched for a few seconds as he just stood in

the driveway. The only car in the yard was his so I

wondered if anyone was even home. From where we were

watching it looked like he was on his phone and that was soon confirmed when my phone went off.

My Everything <3: Sorry I ran out so fast one of the members needed some counseling and it was urgent. Be home soon. Love u!

I couldn't even speak as the tears flowed down my face. This wasn't supposed to be my life but here I was living it. The pain from that text and knowing that my husband was lying to me was unbearable. Never in a million years did I see us getting to this place.

When I first met Gavon when we were younger I knew that I wanted to marry him. Then once we reconnected and he showed me that he was serious I knew that it was meant to be. Now as I watch him ring the doorbell of his ex I was no longer sure of what was meant to be at all.

Shenita snatched the phone from my hand when she noticed me crying. Nothing was making sense to me at the moment and I couldn't find the words to express how I felt

so I just sat there and cried. I wasn't a punk in the least and

when it came down to throwing these hands I would but I

didn't feel like I should have to fight for a man. Especially

one that I shared vows with before God and our families.

"I KNOW YOU LYIN'!" Shenita said clicking

away on my phone as she got out of the truck leaving her

door open.

I got myself together quickly before I followed her.

The last thing I was going to give Chardonnay was the

satisfaction of thinking she had one up on me. Not Chasiti

Cunningham.

Both Shenita and I were moving at a steady pace

towards the house. Instead of coming up right in the front

we eased around to the side of the house where we could

hear and see. I needed to know what they had to talk about

before I went off. I knew good and well that I had told the

both of them not to try me but here they were testing my

gangster. Gavon may have been no longer thuggin' but I was about to show him how I could really get down.

We heard his phone go off and he reached into his pocket a he rang the bell again. Whatever he needed with Chardonnay he was in a hurry to get it. I looked down at the phone in my hand and noticed that Shenita had replied to his text.

Me: I hope it's worth it!!!

Just as he was opening the text the door was opening.

"Aye Char you didn't text me back," Gavon said.

"But I did!" I yelled no longer able to be silent. I had found my voice once again and it was about to be on and poppin'.

At the sound of my voice Gavon, the man that opened the door who I assumed to be this scambooger's husband, and the scambooger herself all looked in my direction.

Had Chardonnay not been pregnant I would have drug her all up and down the steps making sure she hit every step on the way down for that smirk she wore on her face. Gavon looked so stupid that it was almost comical if I was in a laughing mood and her husband was looking mad and confused. One thing about it though Chardonnay knew how to pick a fine man cause her husband was nice on the eyes but he looked sneaky too.

"Wh…wha…what are you doing here baby? Where are the kids?"

"Oh now you worried about your family? Were you worried about them when you high tailed it out of the house and made your way over to your side chick's house?"

"Hold on who you calling a side chick? Just because you got the ring don't mean nothing. I was the first and will be the last."

"Oh word?" both Shenita and her husband said at the same time.

"I know you lyin'! I swea' fo' lawd the only reason I ain't draggin' ya ole bald headed donkey neck behind all up and down dis road is because you carrying that little ugly baybee. But I got you once you drop dat load so you mindaswell be ready to meet me fontatown cause it's gone down!"

Shenita was on ten and that meant so was her accent. She was talking so fast and loud even I had trouble understanding what she was saying. It didn't matter though at this point because the only person that should have been talking was standing in my face looking dumb.

"So this the type of Christian or Pastor you are huh? Sleeping around on your wife with another married woman," her husband said. "Don't think that I didn't know who you were when I came to the church today. I just wanted to see if you could man up and keep it one hunnit since you from the streets and all. I guess everything Char told me about you being weak was true."

"I. KNOW. YOU. LYINNNN'!" Shenita was getting started again. "Lil buddy tried to yay with the yay earlier at the mall. I see why though if this ya ole lady."

"What?"

"He tried to get with me," Shenita said doing the best she could to talk proper.

"Oh so you a chubby chaser too Ken? That's how you livin'?"

"Who she calling chubby? I'm a plush pal,"

"None of this matters! I need to know why my husband is still going behind my back with you after I clearly told him not to try me," I said taking over. This was getting out of hand and I needed some answers. Nothing was making sense and this was all bad.

"Bae can we just go home and talk about this? Let's not do this out here in front of everybody," Gavon finally spoke up.

"We might as well do it out here cause it looks like the three of you have been hiding long enough behind closed doors. For God's sake you're a Pastor Gavon!"

I could feel my pressure rising and my palms getting sweaty. I did my best to calm myself down before I ended up back in the hospital. My doctor told me that I was going to have to stop letting things get to me like they do but this here was sending me over the edge.

"What's poppin' between you and my wife though?" Kendrick asked Gavon.

"Look now is not the time for this. I need to get home and talk to my wife," Gavon said trying to avoid the question. He wasn't about to get off that easy.

"Nah. We don't have nothing to talk about until you answer his question."

"That your baby Gee?" I asked in a voice that even I didn't recognize.

Instead of answering my question I watched Gavon as his eyes left mine and his head dropped. It was at that moment where I felt like my world was over. Everything I thought I knew I didn't and there was no one available to make any of this make sense to me.

Slowly I started to back away once I saw the smirk on Chardonnay's face. Was I just the one that had the ring, his kids, and his last name but she still had his heart? The look in Kendrick's eyes held the same question that mine did. But from what Shenita had just expressed about their encounter he was no better than Gavon.

"Bae please let me explain." Gavon said reaching out for me. I cringed at the thought of him touching me after he had once again been touching Chardonnay. How many times had he come home and kissed me after being with her? The thought made me sick to my stomach as the tears fell and I emptied everything that was locked away in my stomach on the ground beside me.

"You don't owe her an explanation about anything Gavon. You kno-" Chardonnay began but was quickly cut off. Before anyone could prevent it Shenita had reached around both men and slapped Chardonnay clean across her face with the force of a mac truck.

"Open ya mouf again hear? Ooohhh I wish Maw Maw was still here cause I know she turning over in her grave right about now," Shenita said moving Gavon out of the way so she could get to me.

"Oh no," Chardonnay moaned as she grabbed her stomach. I looked up just to see the fluid running down her legs and automatically knew what that meant but that was the least of my concerns.

The fact that my heart felt like it was being crushed in my chest superseded any emotion that I have ever felt as

No More Thuggin

I watched this woman reach her arm out for my husband

and he rushed to be by her side.

Alvin

Dancing around the kitchen I made sure that everything was in place for dinner. Since both Marisa and I had to work the next few days this was the only time that we could get together. We had already gone to church together that morning but parted ways because I wanted to surprise her with dinner. All I gave her was the time to be here and I had everything else under control.

"I don't wanna bore you with my troubles yeah but there's something bout your love that makes me weak and knocks me off my feet," I sang my boy Donell Jones' hit 'Knocks Me Off My Feet' cause that was exactly what Marisa was doing to me the more time I spent with her. She would never replace my late wife and she wasn't trying to. Marisa was simply trying to love me the way God needed her to and that was alright with me.

I looked over at the clock ad saw that she should have been arriving any second so I began to plate the shrimp scampi, steamed broccoli, and garlic bread before pouring the chilled Pinot Grigio into the wine glasses. Just as I had placed the second glass down the doorbell rang.

I checked my appearance real quick before I opened the door. I had to make sure I was looking presentable and for an old cat I was still on point with the swag. My dreads were freshly retwisted and I had gotten lined up the day before. Getting out of my suit that I wore earlier I changed into some navy slacks and a simple white button up shirt. The sleeves had been rolled up to keep me from getting any food on them when I was making the plates so I just left them the way they were. My navy Louis Vuitton loafers with the emblem on the front gave me a casual but dressy feel.

"What's up gorgeous?" I said as soon as I opened the door to look into the face of my future wife.

I didn't care what anyone said about moving too fast. When a man was presented his wife he knew and he would do everything he could to keep her. I was a real romantic and I loved treating my woman good. That's all I knew how to do. Playing the field and sleeping around had never been my thing and I never understood why men felt the need to have a woman at home and then have others out in the streets. That's why it pissed me off how Gavon was handling himself. I know I wasn't here to teach him how to be a man and how to treat a woman but that didn't mean I wasn't going to get him together real soon.

"Hey handsome," Marisa said walking up to me and standing on her tip toes to lightly kiss my lips.

Looking down into her face made me want to marry her right here on the spot. She was absolutely beautiful. The full package. Educated, a hard worker, and she loved just as hard as I did. Things were getting deep between us but there was only one problem. My son. In order to move forward I wanted my son's blessing but any time I went to talk to him about my relationship we would always start arguing or someone interrupted us.

"It smells good in here babe," she said coming inside and sitting her purse on the table by the door.

"What? You thought ya man couldn't cook?" I asked her as I walked behind her.

Stopping in mid stride she brought her hands to her mouth as she looked at the set up I had for her. The table was set and candles were lit on the table. I had some lavender lilies placed in a vase on the table in front of her chair.

"You remembered," she said turning to face me. I guess when she told me her favorite flower she thought I would forget but I made sure that whenever she was talking I listened and paid attention.

"Of course."

Taking her by the hand I walked her closer to the table when she stopped me.

"Oh babe this is my favorite song!"

"Well may I have this dance then?"

"You can have whatever you like as long as you keep treating me like this."

"I'll spend the rest of my life treating you like the queen you are if you let me," I told her as I pulled her close.

Freddie Jackson was singing about needing a little love right now and I was definitely in agreement with him. Being that I had never shared my gift of singing with Marisa I felt like this was the best time to do so.

"Whenever we touch like this whenever I touch your lips baby my heart beats faster by the minute," I sang along.

Pulling away from me with the biggest smile I had ever seen on her face she said, "I didn't know you could sing!"

"It's just a little something. Nothing that will win me an award or anything," I laughed.

Just when we were about to sit down to eat before our food got completely cold there was pounding coming from the other side of my front door.

"Stay right here," I told Marisa. Whoever it was that was beating like that had to have been on ten and I didn't want her in the way. If something jumped off then she would be able to get out of the way. No matter how long I had been out of jail I was still on high alert in some situations. Like I didn't like being in a crowded room and if I didn't have my back to the wall and was able to see all of the exits and what everyone was doing then I wasn't comfortable.

Before I could get to the door to see who it was it came bursting open and in came Gavon looking like a mad man.

"CHASITI! CHASITI! Man just let me explain ma!"

"Whoa son what's going on?" I wanted to know as I watched him go in and out of each room of the house.

"Man Pop I messed up. I messed up big time. Where is Chas? I need to talk to her and make this right," he said still searching high and low.

I stood there knowing that this had Chardonnay all over it and I was finally seeing what Mama Jean would always tell me when she came to visit me. She never had a good thing to say about the girl and once I had gotten out I had never met her because my son was no longer with her. The first time I saw her at the church I knew she was trouble and I tried warning Gavon of that very fact but he was as hard headed as they came.

"Chas isn't here Gee," I told him as I stood in the middle of the living room.

"Where did she go? Did she come by with the babies?" He asked in a panic.

This was alarming to me. To know that my daughter and my grandbabies were missing took me to another level and I knew that whatever it was that he had done was her breaking point.

"What did you do to that girl?"

Gavon didn't answer me right away. He just sat down on the couch with his head in his hands as he bounced his leg up and down.

"She caught me over at Chardonnay's house," he said.

I just knew my ears were playing tricks on me because there was no way that my married son had just told me that his wife had caught him at the house of his ex.

"What on earth were you doing over there? I know I told you to get it together before it got out of hand."

"Chardonnay was texting me and she said that she was hurting in her stomach. I asked where her husband was and she told me that he wasn't home yet. I was trying to give her some pointers on how to ease the pain and time when the pains would hit her. Then when I got home from church I ended up questioning Chasiti about why she met up with Chardonnay."

"You mean to tell me you questioned your wife about another female? One that has the potential to cause your marriage to end? And by the way you are looking she may have just succeeded," I told him without an ounce of sympathy. He had made this bed and now he was going to have to lay in it.

"It wasn't like that Pop."

"Finish telling me what happened."

"Well once she told me off she dropped the subject and began to cook dinner. I was changing so I could go and play with Jean'nae outside when I got another text from Chardonnay saying that the pain was hitting her every six minutes and she was hurting so bad. I told her to call 911 and her husband.

The little dots that popped up letting me know she was typing her response just stopped all of a sudden and when I asked her if she was ok I didn't get a reply. I tried a few more times and when she still hadn't said anything back I got my keys and left out. I just told Chas I would be right back. I swear I was just going over there to make sure she was good and nothing had happened. Her husband opened the door and then Chas and Shenita came out of nowhere and things went left," he finished.

"Nah things went left long before now. They went left the moment you picked up the phone when that girl called you after all this time. Then they kept going the wrong way when you didn't tell your wife. You know Mama Jean always said everything done in the dark will come to the light. You are a man of the cloth for God's sake Gavon! How are you going to lead a household if you can't lead your own home?"

"Listen don't come at me about leading a house when you failed to do that yourself."

Walking up on him I did the best I could to keep my composure.

"Because you are upset I'm going to let you have that. We both know why I was there so we not even going to go that route anymore. You will not continue to hold that over my head. The state has done that for way too long."

"Babe do you want to reschedule? I know this is important and I don't want to intrude on family affairs," Marisa said coming into view from the kitchen. I had completely forgotten that she was still here once Gavon came busting in like SWAT.

"Oh yea? You bring some random up in the house of my dead grandmother who was also your wife's mother?"

"What you will do is respect me and my lady. I'm not the one with a wife that I'm cheating on."

Before I knew it Gavon had hit me with a quick two piece and I lost it. If he wanted to get down then his wish was my command.

No More Thuggin

Chasiti

Lil' Gavon was crying uncontrollably. Jean'nae was asking where we were going and where her daddy was at. Everything was too overwhelming right now. To see Gavon run to Chardonnay's side really hurt me deeply. Shenita and I headed home but the cops came to pick her up for assault. I texted Gavon from her phone letting him know she needed to be bailed out. I packed all me and my children clothes and walked out. It was hard for me to and the whole time I packed tears were running down my face. I left my cell phone on the nightstand so Gavon wouldn't be able to contact me. My Papa made sure I had plenty of money so I would just go and get another one tomorrow. I wasn't running away like most girls do, I was leaving until I could think straight. I never want to keep Gavon from his kids but he wasn't thinking correctly and he made his decision in the front of Chardonnay's house who he wanted

to be with.

I pulled around to the back of my old house I grew

up in. My Papa had an old shed in the back that was rigged

so I parked my car inside and got the kids out. Gavon

hadn't been on this side in so long I'm pretty sure he

wouldn't check here. When I used my key to enter I smiled

at the smell of my Papa's house. He was away on a small

vacation and I knew he was going to flip when he got back

and we were there. He gave Gavon one warning and that

was to never disrespect our marriage.

"Mama I'm hungry," Jean'nae said.

"Give me just a second to get your brother situated

and I'll fix you something."

I turned the TV on for Jean'nae as I settled Lil'

Gavon for his nap. I knew my Papa had plenty of food so I

planned on whipping up something real good. Most of the

time when I was frustrated or aggravated I used that time to cook. I taught myself how to cook some of the most exquisite dishes. I missed hearing Shenita's voice and I wanted to know if she was okay. I picked Papa's cordless phone up and dialed her New Orleans number.

"Hey baybee! Where ya at? Gavon watching me like a hawk trying to figure out if I know something chile."

"How you know this me Shenita?"

"Guh ain't nobody else calling me from no 912 numba."

"Yea you right. How is he," I asked as I pulled some Bubba burgers out of the freezer. I planned to fry them up with some grilled onions and gravy.

"Well Chas he ain't doing too good. He dropped me earlier today and burned out of here before I could get in the house good enough."

"Who is that?" I heard Gavon through the phone.

"I know you lyin' asking me about my phone," Shenita fussed as I listened.

"I thought it was my wife that's all."

"Nah bruh this ain't yo wife."

Shenita sat on the phone silently for minute.

"Guh I got to go cause he got a feeling this you. I'll talk to you tomorrow," Shenita hung up before I could respond.

I placed the cordless phone back and continued to cook dinner. After finishing I got Jean'nae plate fixed and fed Lil' Gavon before I sat down to eat. I was so exhausted from the events from today that I wanted to shower and go to sleep. I had two days before my Papa returned. I wanted to have this thing with Gavon worked out by then but I knew it wasn't going to work out that way. Walking through the house I checked on Jean'nae to make sure was in bed sleep before I went to lay with my son. I had him trained to sleep in his bed but he didn't have one here so he would have to sleep in the bed with me. If Mama Jean was here she would swear he would die from SIDS.

Lil' Gavon wiggling in his sleep woke me up. Since becoming a mother I was used to light sleep. I opened my eyes to see Lil' Gavon just staring at me. I placed him in the bend of my arm and closed my eyes. Taking in a deep breath a fragrance caught me. It was a fragrance only my husband with wear because I bought it. I raised my head up and didn't see him in the room. I laid back down but the scent of Chrome filling the room. It was so strong that I laid my son back down and sat on the side of the bed. I placed my feet in my fluffy bedroom shoes and raised up from the bed.

"Where you going?"

Gavon was laying on the floor at the foot of the bed. I stood there just staring at him trying to figure out how he got in the house and how did he even think to check here out of all places.

"Why are you here Gee? Shouldn't you be at the hospital with your new baby?" I asked walking out of the bedroom into the hall.

"Chas don't walk away from me without letting me explain the situation."

I popped my lips and continued to walk up the hall to get away from the kids. The last thing I wanted to Jean'nae to wake up and see is her parents arguing.

"Chasiti!"

"Gavon lower your voice in this house. Our kids are sleeping," I told him over my shoulder. It wasn't long before Gavon grabbed my gown stopping me in my tracks. We never argued but he always told me that he never liked when some walked away from him. I turned around and yanked my gown out of his grip.

Throwing his hands up in a surrendering way he continued to walk behind me until we reached the living room.

"Chasiti all I'm asking as your husband is that you hear me out. Everything ain't what it seems. You going off of impulse and what you think you saw."

"From the way Chardonnay was talking, I wasn't going off of just impulse Gee."

"Really Chas? Chardonnay? She live for drama. Yea she got saved but that area of her life ain't delivered yet. She'll do anything to see you squirm," Gavon told me.

"Well since you broke into my Papa house I might as well hear what you got to say," I folded my arms across my chest.

"I have not been with Chardonnay in any sexual way PERIOD! I was just being a friend. Yea I was wrong for that. I know I should've told you but I knew you were going to leave me. The only reason I was over there was because we were texting and she complained about hurting. Being that I was a father of two I was talking her through it.

I suggested she call her husband and 911. When she stop texting I got worried and went over there."

"So you was being a friend. Do you know you being a friend caused a rift in our marriage Gee. I'm your wife, you could've told me she was having marriage problems. So what's the issue with you not answering me about that being your baby?"

"I can't be telling you her issue Chas all I can reassure you is that the baby is not mine," Gavon said.

"You could've fooled me," I said with an attitude.

"Look baby y'all need to come home. No more secrets on my end. I got a lot of kinks I need to work out in my life and I can't do it without you."

I turned the lamp on in the living room and Gavon's face caused me to jump.

"What happened to your face?" I assessed his bruises.

"My Pops."

"What did you do? Your dad doesn't just go off like that."

"He had that broad over there in Mama Jean's house. Then has the nerve to get all puffed up with me cause I decided to call him on it."

"Gee you can't do that. Mama Jean left that house to him. It is now his house. You've really got to let go of your mama Gavon. I know you don't like hearing talk about it but it's time for you to release that part of your life. I bet if you could talk to your mama she would tell you she was fine with your Pops moving on. Nobody wants their spouse to just sit around and be lonely."

"Enough of that. You coming home or nah," he grabbed me and hugged.

"Gavon you got a lot of work to do. Her husband mad and you got your Pops mad at you boy I'm telling you."

Chardonnay

I had my daughter Kendal ten weeks early. I stood in the nursery rubbing her little feet. She had a little pulse monitor hooked up to her little red feet. I felt so alone. Once I got on the ambulance Gavon was gone. Kendrick left right after Chasiti left with Gavon's ghetto cousin. I had her behind locked up for slapping me. I hated the fact I couldn't the heifer back. But as soon as I got out this hospital I was going to find her.

I walked back down to my room to call Kendrick again. I desperately needed to talk to him about Kendal. I laid back in my hospital bed and threw the cover over my legs before I grabbed my phone off of the bedside table and dialed Kendrick's number. As usual the voicemail picked up.

"Hey Ken I was calling to tell you that I had the baby. She's so pretty. I umm really need to talk to you about something. Call me back or just come up here to Memorial and see us. I'm in room 348." My tears started to fall before I could finish my message so I hung up abruptly.

My next call was to Gavon. I was glad he decided to stay with me until the ambulance came. It made me feel good that he choose to stay with me and let his wife fluffy tail running off. I put the phone to my ear as it started ringing. The phone picked up and started talking.

"Hey Gee, I had the baby."

"Annnnddd. What that got to do with my husband?"

"So I guess you went running back cause big girls like you need a man."

"I know she didn't. Give me the tha phone," I could hear Shenita geechee talking self.

"No baby I never run back. Gavon came running after me. And I know that baby is not my husband's better yet he told me everything. I suggest you find someone else to play with white wine."

"I'm not about to sit here and argue with you. I called to talk to Gavon but I see he done got soft by letting his wife answer the phone now. Tell him I'll see him once I'm released tomorrow."

"Guh bye! With yo jealous self," Chasiti hung up in my face.

I placed the phone back down on the bedside table and laid back in the bed. I hated my life right now. It was so hard to get a man to love me. When Gavon first started kicking it with me it was innocent but my feelings started to get in the way. I still loved Kendrick but I wanted Gavon just a little. It was some of Gavon features I wished my husband had. Maybe I was jealous of Chasiti because she could get her man to chase after her and I couldn't get mine to even pick up his phone.

I opened my eyes and looked around my room. The loneliness I was feeling was making me real gloomy. I was starting to question myself and my marriage. I hated bringing my daughter in the middle of this and she was already sick. Today was the day they were letting me go home and I had to leave my baby here until she was well enough to go home.

The nurse came in and let me take a shower and helped me pack up. I called Kendrick because I needed a ride and he was riding around in my car. Again he didn't answer so for the next five hours I sat in the nursery trying to bond with my baby as much as possible. The shift was getting to change so I decided to call a cab and head home. I only had a few dollars on me since everything happen so fast I wasn't prepared. I paid the cab driver and lugged my bags into my house.

I knew Kendrick had been staying home by the way the house looked. He had a pair of shoes in the living room. The kitchen was a hot mess and our bedroom smelled like his work clothes. Because I didn't like a nasty house I decided before I got some rest to clean up. Once I had my house smelling like Pine-Sol I was satisfied. I went into Kendal's room and decided to get things organized in there too.

Hearing the door chime I prepared myself for the worse as I heard Kendrick throw the keys on the table. I could hear his heavy boots walking up the hall as my breath got caught in my throat. All this time I been calling him and now I was face to face with him since our incident in the front yard. He looked in Kendal's room at me and kept walking into our bedroom. I finished folding one of the onesies and placed in the drawer before heading behind him. I didn't want to argue with him but I needed to talk to him and see where his head was at. When I entered the room he was sitting on the side of the bed with his phone in his hand.

"Kendrick why haven't you been answering my calls?"

He ignored me and kept doing whatever it was he was doing on his phone. I had to take a breather because I didn't want to turn up on him.

"Kendrick did you hear me," I stepped right in front him. I could tell I made him uncomfortable because I was all in his space due to the nudge he gave me.

"Watch out Chardonnay," he said.

"Okay so you can hear. Where have you been and have you not been answering your phone? I'm still your wife Kendrick."

"Not for long," he looked up at me with anger in his eyes.

"Wha- what you mean by that?"

"I mean I don't think we need to be married anymore. You stood right in my face the other day and embarrassed me. You still love Gavon Stevie Wonder can see it. So since you want to be with him, I'm gone let y'all have that little bit and I'm going to head back to the Carolina's."

"Ken it's not even like that. I was saying that to hurt his wife."

"Did you think about hurting me Chardonnay? I guess that didn't cross your mind."

"Ken don't play innocent you was trying to holla at the big amazon girl did you not think that hurt me?"

"Look ma, this what we going to do. I'm going my way and you go your way. I'm sorry we even tried to keep this mess of a marriage going."

"Ken I really need to talk to you about the baby. She really needs you."

Kendrick stood up and towered over me, "That's not my baby." With that he went into the closet and started packing.

"Kendrick the baby is yours. I promise! We can do a paternity test or whatever. You can't leave like this. I need you and your daughter needs you," I tried to pull on his arm.

"Give me some time Chardonnay. I need some space to think," Kendrick snatched his arm.

"What you mean some time. That's all I've been giving you is time and space to sleep around. It's like no matter where I take you, you always find some chick to lay up with. I've apologized and that's just not good enough for you. But you been apologizing since we been together and I still stuck it out with you."

Kendrick just stood there staring at me with a blank expression that I couldn't understand. His daughter was fighting for life while he stood in front of me wanting some space.

"I don't know what you want me to tell you," Kendrick continued to walk towards the door.

"You know what. You can leave but you can't take my car. I need to be able to see our daughter and I can't do that if her father is out laying up with another woman in my car."

Kendrick threw the keys at me and left out the door. I stood at the door and watched him walk down the street like he was from Savannah. I placed my hand on my head because I still didn't tell him about our daughter. I just had too much going on.

Kendrick

I was so mad Chardonnay I didn't care about walking as long as I was away from her. Yea I was a man and yes I cheated but for my wife to sit there and practically admit to still be in love with another man broke me. I was trying so hard to change but I was a sucker for a cute face, pretty teeth and nice feet.

I walked for so long I ended up at Memorial. I stood in the window staring at a tiny baby that resembled my sister before her health problems claimed her life at the age of thirteen. Between Down syndrome and spinal bifida she didn't stand a chance in this cruel world.

As I watched the machine breathe for baby girl who name card read Kendal, I wondered why Chardonnay never mentioned to me that the baby had Down Syndrome. She was so busy arguing with me that she failed to mention the birth defects the baby had. I wanted to so badly touch her but decided not to get too attach knowing she wasn't going to make past this point. My mind was even telling she wasn't mine.

The more I stared at her the more I thought about watching my sister take her last breaths. I could still remember my mama crying and wiping my sister's face because her mouth was dry from dehydration. She could no longer get feedings in her g-tube. I was fifteen years old and I felt like my world ended when my sister left. I always had a soft for anyone developmental disabilities, it wasn't their fault. After battling with myself I decided to go to the nurse's station and ask to go in the nursery. If Kendal was my baby I definitely wanted her to know her daddy's touch.

"Hey is there any way I can go in the nursery and spend time with baby girl Kendal?"

"What's your name?" The nurse asked me.

"Kendrick Anderson," I responded.

"Okay yes. You are on the list. Let me get you a band to go on your arm that way you can go back there as much as you want," she busied herself getting the band together.

I was shocked Chardonnay even put my on the paperwork with her hateful self. The nurse got done with my band and placed it on my arm with my wedding band on it.

"It's nice to see a young man come up her and spend time with their child. So many babies don't know their father's voices. What's even better is that you're married. It's nothing like raising a family with the one you love. Ms. Kendal is going to be a diva so you get ready daddy," the nurse laughed and buzzed me into the nursery.

Putting sanitizer on my hands, I walked up to her little bed. She was laying there with her little eyes open and it made me smile. I wanted to be a father but never really knew how being that my mama raised me. I placed my hand in the hole to touch her feet. The light that was shining on her was keeping her warm. The little diaper that was wrapped around her covered half of her body. Her hair was slicked down on her head and she barely had any eyelashes. I didn't want to make Chardonnay take a blood test put in order to move forward I needed clarity.

"Thank you for coming," Chardonnay walked up behind me.

I turned around and got ready to walk out because I didn't want to cause a scene in the hospital. Chardonnay still couldn't be trusted.

"Why you leaving?"

I bent down so only she could hear me, "Set up the paternity test and then holla at me." With that I undressed out of the hospital gown that was covering my clothes and walked out the door.

Thankfully I was off for two days so I decided to just go and check into a hotel room. Now that Kendal was here I couldn't just up and move back to the Carolina's and leave her here for her crazy mama to take care of her. I knew how to take care of her if she came home because I took care of my sister. Just thinking of her made me take my cell phone out and call my mama. My mama was a street chick. She still ran the streets but she never neglected us when we were younger. My sister had some of the best care when she was living. My mama went out and hustled every day.

"Aye ma. What's up?"

"Ain't nothing son. Chilling on the porch smoking and kicking the bobo with my homeboys Reno and Dan. What you doing?"

"Nothing I was just thinking about you and Zena."

"Nah son you ain't sounding right. What's going on? Do I need to drive to Georgia I'm only up the road," she said into the phone.

"Chardonnay had the baby ma. She premature and I don't think she going to make man. Me and Chardonnay ain't kicking like that no more."

"Stop talking like that. I didn't raise you that way. And what you mean you and your wife not kicking it? Y'all married."

"She look just like Zena mama. She's beautiful."

"Don't ignore me boy. You heard me ask you about you and your wife and you just flew right over that. Listen son my grandbaby going to make. I'm gon' drive down that way with Reno nem' this week so I can spend time with y'all."

"Alright mama, just hit me up when you get here."

"Yea," she said before hanging up the phone.

I needed to clear my head but it was hard to get around without a car. I couldn't keep spending money on taxes. Maybe I needed to dip into my little stash and buy me a car. I was trying to avoid Chardonnay at all cost but I had to go home and at least get some clothes. But who I

wasn't avoiding was Gavon Cunningham. Wherever I

caught him it was going to be me and him.

No More Thuggin

Alvin

"Alvin baby calm down," Marisa said playing in my
hair.

"Marisa I've worked too hard to try and stay out of
prison. You know if you wasn't there that fight could've
got out of hand. I don't know why I let that boy get me
worked up like that."

"I don't know either? It's been a few days now Al
and you still worked up. I understand where Gavon is
coming from that's why it doesn't bother me when he acts
out. When I was his age I did the same thing to my mother.
I was a daddy's girl and when he passed suddenly and she
tried to move on I wasn't having it. It was until I walked in
on her crying on one of my weekly visits because she was
lonely. I was being real selfish. But I had to realize that.
Now you got to let Gavon realize it. All these years later

my mother is still happily married and he treats her like gold."

Listening to Marisa made me realize now why Gavon was so hurt. Yea he verbalized it, but it was always out of anger.

"I think you need to reach out to him," Marisa said raising my head off her lap.

"I'll think about it," I said nonchalantly.

"Well I'm heading to work. I'll call you on my break. It's baby season so there's no telling when I'll catch a break," Marisa explained.

"I kissed her on her lips and walked her to the door. I was staying at her place until things calmed down.

I still was uncomfortable being in someone else's house. I was thankful for my house but I didn't want Gavon popping up with air in his chest. Next time he was going to leave with more than black eye. I missed my wife Danielle but I had to move on. If I continued to put everyone else first then I would never be happy. I was going to take Marisa advice and talk to Gavon. I prayed he got his little situation taken care of so he wouldn't be so hostile with me. I tried to tell that boy that this was going to catch up with him. Chardonnay was a messy type of broad. I could smell her crap a mile away. From the look in her eyes she was working all her magic to get my son wrapped up in her web.

I hadn't seen my grandkids in a few days I wasn't ready to go over there but I did want to see if Chasiti would let me see them. I decided to give her a call and see what was up with her and my son as well.

"Hey Pops," Chasiti sung in the phone.

I pulled my ear away because if she was splitting up with Gavon she surely sound happy about it.

"What you doing baby girl? I wanted to see the kids if it's cool with you. I know you and Gavon got a lot going on and I don't want to intervene with that. I know you heard about our incident," I told her over the phone.

"Pops you know you can see these kids. Jean'nae been begging to see you. And yes I saw Gavon's face. Y'all really need to get this right it's too many people depending on both of y'all. My kids being one. I understand both sides and to be honest I'm on your side and I've been talking to him about it," she whispered in the phone.

"You sound just like Marisa. I'll come around to it. I want him to be calm before I approach him about talking."

I hung up the phone with Chasiti and decided to cook myself something to eat and lounge. Being on the truck all day made my knees ache so whenever I could get a minute to prop them I took it. As I enjoyed my food I stared out the window and thought of a plan to get to my son.

Gavon

"Chasiti you need to put your J's on today baby. You already know how praise and worship go. We go hard in there, you going trying to be all cute with your flats on."

I watched as Chasiti went back in the closet and came out with her J's and jeans on. I had a new praise and worship leader that would have you crunk and then take you right into worship like he wasn't just rapping. I loved my churched and the freedom we had to bring God's word.

"Is this better?"

"Yep that's better."

"So what's up with you and Pops?" Chasiti snuck in.

"Look now I'm trying to go to church with a clear mind. I don't need nothing hindering me. I finally feel free from all the drama going on so I just want to preach and come on."

"Gee you just sweeping stuff under the rug. Your rug is getting higher and higher. It's so much stuff under that rug won't nothing else fit," Chasiti said.

I heard her but I decided to ignore her and make sure Shenita was getting Lil' Gavon ready.

"I don't kno why you got me going to church. Lordt I hope the place don't burn down when I step in dere. Why you making me go doe?" She asked with an attitude.

"Shenita you ain't been to church since you been here. You know if Mama Jean was living you would have that wool on with you white ruffle socks and two ponytails."

"Chile Maw Maw had me hot with her every Sunday. Unlike you I don't like church."

"Why?"

"Cause we don't do this over in Nawlins'. Every time I come to Georgia y'all in church. Do y'all do anything else?"

"Shenita you too old to still be like that. My church is not like any other. I bet you any amount of money you'll love it."

"Aight. If I don't you got to eat gumbo," she laughed and stuck he tongue out.

I hated gumbo and Shenita knew it. But I knew she was going to enjoy it. I got the bag ready for the baby and some snacks for Jean'nae so she won't drive her mama crazy.

"Alright I'm about to head out. I'll see y'all there." I kissed Chasiti and the kids and then mushed Shenita in the side of her head.

I headed to the church ahead of everyone else so I could make sure everything was set up right. I want to make sure the sound was working right and I had plenty of bottle of waters to go around. I had some music playing as I made sure there were enough chairs at each table when I heard the door close. I looked up to see my Pops standing there staring back at me.

"Wassup son?" He held his hand out. I stood there staring at him. I had to get myself together and I needed to do it quick.

"Why you here," I mugged him.

"Take the air out your chest son. I ain't even here for all that. I just wanted to talk to you before church started. I'm here so you can say whatever you need to say to me about Marisa."

"It's not Marisa I have the problem with, it's you. How can you say you love someone but you ready to move on?"

"Son is your mama here? No! And I can't bring her back. If I could then we wouldn't be here now would we? I loved my wife boy. Believe it or not Marisa knows the love I carry for your mama. That will never leave me but I can't be lonely for the rest of my life while everyone around me living a happy life."

I sat down at one of the tables. He was spitting truth and I had to bow down to the truth. I rested my head in my hands and went into a deep thought.

"I plan to marry Marisa but she won't let me move on without getting my relationship with you right first. So have you said everything you needed to say?"

"I want to sit down and talk with Marisa. If y'all getting married then that means my kids will be around her. I don't really know her like that."

"That's cool with me son. I'm about to get my seat for church I see you got people getting here early."

I got up to meet some of the dudes coming in from the streets. Savannah was vicious but it amazed me how some of the dudes will stop gang banging to come to church for an hour. I did as much as I could within that hour. Whatever I was doing it was working because they were becoming consistent.

Chasiti called me to let me know she was outside with the kids. I went and helped her with the kids and walked them in. Instead of Shenita keeping her mind clean she saw all the brothers in here looking like thugs and got turned on.

"Shenita get your mind right."

"Gee leave me lone. You didn't tell me you was doing it like dis. Baybee these men fione you hear me. Yes gawd," she said fanning herself.

"Sit down! This is not the place for all that. This is a church and I need you to act like you got some sense."

"Get out my face Gee. I'll be good until we walk outside that door. I got my eye on one of them and he ain't got no ring on either."

"Stop it," Chasiti told Shenita.

I shook my head and headed towards the back so I can get my wireless mic put on my shirt. I could hear my boy Tone getting the people prepared for a crazy praise. I stood in front of the mirror and bowed my head and prayed. I always wanted to be free when I preached. Today I was going to tell the church how I almost lost my family. I prayed that this would help some of the other brothers in the church realize what they got. I was trying to get everything on track at home so I got my number changed so Chardonnay couldn't make contact with me.

"Aye bruh you got somebody on the church phone wanna holla you," Kareem stuck his head in the door.

I walked over to my little desk and picked the phone up.

"Hello?"

"Why you changed your number on me?" Chardonnay yelled in the phone.

"Chardonnay I told you man I'm done. I'm trying to get this thing right with my wife. You stay on that messy mess and I ain't got time for it."

"Kendrick left me Gavon and I really need your help."

"I can't help you anymore Chardonnay. How about I get my wife to come along with me?"

"Nope she can't step foot around me period."

"Just like I thought. Chardonnay I got to go church about to start," I hung up the phone in her face and headed out to the stage.

The church was packed. It held over 50 tables with at least six chairs to a table. Every chair was full. I opened my tablet and started my message. The response I was getting from my message was good. Once I got to the end I called all my men to the front so I could pray for them. I hadn't even gave them my testimony yet because I didn't feel led too. As I moved closer to the edge of the stage I could feel my leg being pulled. Before I could walk away I was being snatched off the stage by Kendrick Anderson himself.

Alvin

Now one thing I wasn't going to do was sit back and let somebody catch my son off guard. I looked over at Chasiti as she held Jean'nae's hand and held on to Lil' Gavon tightly.

"Go in Gavon's office with them kids right now," I told Chasiti before making my way up to Gavon. By the time I made it up there the whole hood was stomping this dude out. Gavon wasn't even the one on the ground. He was trying to get everybody else off of the cat that came in here with the foolishness.

A sound of a small gun going off caused everyone to scatter.

"So wassup? Who in here tryin' to pop off doe?" Shenita pointed the gun in the air again.

"Shenita where you get that from?" I asked her.

"Oh unc I been havin' dese. I'm from Nawlins' and I never kno' when I may have to correct somebody."

I could tell Shenita was upset because her accent was very strong and she was talking faster than I could understand.

"Give me the gun Nita."

"Nah! I'll give it to you when they clear out the way so I can see my cousin."

"I'm right here Nita. I'm good give me the gun," Gavon said.

"Who dis coward coming in here starting mess? Did his mamma n'em not teach him any better," Shenita said trying to look and see who the dude was laying on the ground.

"Aye Pops get her cooled down while I call the paramedics to come get this dude. He in the wrong hood trying to jump on me and we at church," Gavon said walking off shaking his head.

I walked Shenita down to the office to sit with Chasiti and the kids. Shenita was hesitant about giving me the gun but after Chasiti talked to her she decided to hand it over. After securing them in the office I walked back out to where Gavon was. They were circled around the dude laying on the floor. He had the nerve to be snoring so I knew they had put him to sleep. It shouldn't have been but it was funny and I knew that if Reno was here, that would've been his first move.

"So who is this cat?" I asked walking back up to the small crowd.

"Chardonnay's husband," Gavon said intertwining his hands on the top of his head. That was his go to move when he was beyond stressed and didn't know what he could do to resolve the situation he was faced with.

"Why you looking so worried that he came in here," I asked.

"This is a church Pop and I'm trying to steer clear of any trouble. What will this look like to the community when it gets out? And besides who gone call that girl and tell her that her husband in the hospital? I'm not doing it. I just got back right with my baby," Gavon told me.

"Alright Gee we got to get outta here before 12 get here. We all probably got warrants. Holla at us if you need anything," one of the new members said. He was still trying to get right.

I watched as about ten or fifteen of my members headed out the front door as the sirens got closer and shook my head. I knew this wasn't what my son had signed up for. He was supposed to be bringing them away from that lifestyle and mentality and here they were acting the same way in church as they would outside of it. God was seriously needed.

"I'll call her," Chasiti said behind us.

"Nah bae. I can't let you do that."

"I got it Gee, seriously," she said walking over to him. Looking into her eyes I knew that she was the one for my son. After all of the unnecessary things he had put her through she still had her man's back.

The paramedics came in and placed Chardonnay's husband on the stretcher as the police came in and got a report from Gavon. I knew he wasn't going to press charges on dude and surely he wasn't going to tell what really happened.

My phone buzzed in my pocket taking me away from the moment and I knew it was my baby Marisa. I excused myself so I could get a quick talk in with her. She was on call and I had to work for the rest of the week so we tried to talk as much as possible on the phone.

"So how did it go?" Marisa asked.

"Well the talk went well but we had a little altercation not too long ago," I explained.

"Al what did you do?"

"It wasn't me and him baby. It was his ex-girlfriend's husband."

"So what happened? He came in the church and showed out huh? Did Gavon get with him?"

"Look at you with your tea cup out. Y'all women kill me," I laughed.

"I'm just saying it's a lot that go on in the church," she said.

"Well did you think about what I asked you?" Ignoring her million and one questions.

"Alvin I don't think Gavon is going to want that."

"Look you give me an answer and I'll handle the backend of everything else."

"I'll have one for you when you get off. I have to go before my boss starts looking at me over her glasses."

"Alright I love you."

"I love you too Al."

"Now ain't that sweet. Pops in love and talking sweet on the phone," Gavon said with a smirk on his face.

"Wait Pops before you head to work head over to the house and eat dinner with us. Reno and Dan should be almost here and it will be a big family reunion again," Chasiti said.

There was no way that I could skip out on this dinner. I missed those cats something terrible. After burning that boy and his daddy in the car they just took off running only coming home for a few days at a time. I knew it wasn't right but I didn't blame them for what they did. I spent most of my life in prison because of a crime I didn't do and to see the man responsible for killing my wife and taking me away from my son die at the hands of her brothers felt good. No it wasn't right but God was still dealing with me on that part.

"Alright let me get my stuff together and I'll head over," I told them before we went our separate ways.

No More Thuggin

Chardonnay

Kendrick was working my last nerve. Our daughter was finally able to take her first bottle and I wanted Kendrick to be there but just like always he wasn't answering the phone. After so many hours I finally decided to head home for day because I was tired. By the time I made it in my driveway my Bluetooth in my car was going off. I hit the talk button on my steering wheel hoping it was Kendrick calling me from an unknown number.

"Where you at Kendrick?" I said through the speakers.

"Hey Chardonnay this is Chasiti."

"Why the hel-."

"Look we not doing this today. I didn't call you to argue and fuss," she said sounding weary.

"Then what do you want because you got about half a second to talk before you get the operator."

There was a silent pause and I thought she had hung up.

"You there cause your time up," I said.

"Yea I'm here. I'm just trying to make sure that God steps in before my flesh takes over and causes me to go all the way in on you. Being nasty and don't even know what's going on right now. Anyway, your husband is in the hospital and needs you."

"And how would you know that? Let me guess. He was over there with the plush pal gang and y'all squished him," I busted out laughing.

"That's real funny coming from someone that had to use wild grow to grow their edges back. Now since you got some you want to use edge control to slick them beady bees down. Go check on your husband instead always trying to insult me," she hung up unbothered.

I hit the end button on my steering wheel and tried to call Kendrick again but his voicemail picked up. Instead of going back in the house I started the car back up and headed back towards the hospital. After it took me almost twenty minutes of following people around the parking lot I finally got a spot close enough. I walked up to the ER nurses desk with not a bit of concern on my face.

"Hi could you tell me where Kendrick Anderson is," I said as politely as possible.

The receptionist tapped on a few keys before she was able to locate his information. I was beginning to wonder if Chasiti was lying until the nurse spoke.

"Yes he's on the second floor in room 222," she said.

"Thank you."

I walked towards the elevators and headed up to my husband's room. I don't know why my stomach was doing flips. I guess because I didn't know the condition he was in and why he was even in the hospital in the first place. And why was Chasiti calling to tell me about my man. I pushed the door open and he was lying there asleep.

"Kendrick," I pushed him real hard. He woke up groggy so I knew they had him doped up. He had a knot on his head the size of a golf ball. Because of his bright complexion you could see all of his bruises. He opened his eyes slightly and tried his best to focus on my face.

"Kendrick what happened?" I asked him nudging him again. I didn't care about how much pain he was in. It served him right. He was probably out with one of his jump offs and her man caught them.

"Chardonnay go head on now. I'm not in the mood," he said with his eyes rolling.

"I'm not going anywhere until you tell me what happened," I pulled the cover back to see he had a cast on him arm.

"Your man did it."

"Ken they must have given you some good meds cause you sound high. You know you're my man."

"Nah ma, I *was* your man. You be on that drama mess and I'm sick of it. Get, get gone." Kendrick waved me off.

"You's a dumb ungrateful bastard Kendrick. I thought me being here for your dumb behind would open your eyes but I see you still want to be childish. I should have stayed at home when Chasiti called me. I'll have all your stuff packed so whenever you and that raggedy arm of yours get better come get your stuff out of my house."

"Don't worry. My mama on the way here now she'll come get it."

I looked at him with tears in my eyes. I had just had his child a few days ago and he was ready to take the first thing smoking out of here. I couldn't have been that bad of a wife that we couldn't get things right. But if he wanted to leave then he could be my guest.

As soon as I got home I turned my music up and I started packing Kendrick's stuff. I couldn't keep going through this with men. After they used me how they wanted to, they threw me away like trash. I wiped the tears from my eyes as Uncle Sam sung through the speakers. A few hours later I had placed the last of his stuff by the front door and decided to take shower and go to bed. I was too stressed out to deal with anything or anyone else today.

Gavon

"Aye Nita pass me them greens," I said.

We were all sitting around the table indulging in my wife's Sunday dinner. The girl could really throw down, Mama Jean taught her a lot but I was never really there to notice because I was out running the streets.

"Stop looking at your watch your dad and uncle will be here any minute," Chasiti told Shenita.

"I know dat. I'm saying y'all could've waited on my daddy to get here before y'all started eating," Shenita complained.

"Shut up whining big baby. I didn't even wait on my own daddy. Baby this chicken good. God blessed this chicken," I said as I bit the thigh. Chasiti knew I liked my chicken fried extra hard and my skin crispy and she got it right every time.

I had wiped my hands on my napkin just as my door chimed and booming voices came through the house. Shenita hopped up like a little school girl.

"HEY DEDDY!" Shenita yelled like a three year old.

"What's up baby girl? You still thuggin it out down there in New Orleans?" Reno asked his only daughter. It was like looking at the future Jean'nae and myself and I couldn't help but to laugh.

"You know it," she said.

I stood to dap up my uncle Dan and then Reno. I noticed they had a female companion with them. Back in the day my uncles were known for being with different women and she looked just as thugged out as they were so I knew neither one of them was with her on that level. My uncle Reno saw me looking crazy and decided to do the introductions.

"Nephew this here is Rochelle."

"Nice to meet you Rochelle. What you doing with these two crazy dudes?" I said as I nodded my head before giving her a slight hug.

"They cool people," she said. She was pretty but thuggish at the same time. She put you in the mind of the rapper Da Brat but she was a little more feminine than Brat was. Still she wore a fresh out the box pair of Jordan's, ripped boyfriend jeans and Jordan shirt. Her hair was in a nice bob and she sported a tattoo on her neck. Her lips were almost purple in color so I knew she was a smoker. People said that the eyes were the window to the soul but I say if you smoked your lips told.

"Y'all come on in and have a seat. Go ahead and get to eating cause we've started already," Chasiti broke my trance.

"Man look at my great nephew and niece. Chasiti what you feeding my babies?" Dan asked.

"Nope that's your niece Shenita feeding them all this New Orleans food."

"She good for trying to feed all that nasty spicy food," Reno said.

"It wasn't nasty when my mama was cooking it for you," Shenita said rolling her eyes and sticking out her tongue.

"You ain't to grown," Reno said.

"So what's been up with y'all Unc?" I asked Dan.

"I'm thinking about coming home nephew. I'm getting tired."

"What you mean you getting tired," Reno asked.

"Man I been thinking about joining Gee and seeing what this Christ life all about. This other side wearing me down man. My health getting bad bruh. I can't be thuggin with shortness of breath and bad knees we gone get caught," Dan said causing everyone to laugh except Reno.

"Unc I don't know if you want to join Gee. He had the whole hood in there throwing them thangs in church today and if you would've been there you would've bodied the dude. It was so bad I had to let off a shot in there," Shenita said. She had gotten hype all over again.

"You let someone come in the church and chump you nephew? Where he at?" Reno wanted to know.

"Nah he tried too but I got a church full of goons that want to change but haven't completely let the streets go yet. They did what came most natural to them at the moment. Oh boy ended up in the hospital."

"That's my nephew," Reno smiled.

"Who is this cat?" Dan asked.

"Y'all remember my ex Chardonnay?"

"The one Mama said was bald headed? Man she used to give it to her every time she saw her," Uncle Reno said causing everyone to laugh.

"Well it's her husband," I stated.

"Umm excuse me. I don't mean to butt into family stuff but could you tell me what Chardonnay's husband's name is," Rochelle said placing her fork down. Her whole mood changed from lively to ready to pop off real quick and we all picked up on it.

"Some dude named Kendrick something," Shenita said.

Before we knew it Rochelle was pointing a gun at me.

Kendrick

Sitting up in my hospital bed was a struggle. Between the meds and the whipping that I received down at the church I was moving at a snail's pace. The stiffness in my body wouldn't allow me to move any faster. Just thinking about how it all went down made me mad all over again and I knew it would only be a matter of time before I saw Gavon again. I let my emotions get the best of me and that caused me to react without thinking of the consequences of being on his turf.

Shaking off the thoughts I got myself together so that I could make my way down to the nursery. Earlier I had requested that a wheel chair be brought in so that I could go and come as I pleased. I hated not being in control of when I came and when I went. That's the main reason why it shocked even me that I had gotten married.

No More Thuggin

I can't lie and say that when I met Chardonnay that I didn't fall for her. In actuality she was the first woman that I ever fell in love with on the real. When we met I knew she was a little broken but she held her own and knew what she wanted. Everything she had told me she'd gone through made me want to make her life better and for a while I had done just that.

Chardonnay was the one who brought me in to the church and I wanted nothing more than to see what kind of life I could live for God but my appetite for women wouldn't allow me to be all in.

For a while I was able to curve every woman that stepped to me but Chardonnay was the type of woman who had trust issues. No matter what I did right she would always accuse me of doing wrong until I finally got tired of the accusations and acted on them. From that point on everything I thought I wanted was the furthest thing from my mind.

Opening the door to the nursery after I had made sure to put on the sterile gown and sanitize my hands I headed over to the incubator that held little Kendal. The more I looked at her the angrier I felt myself getting. Not at her but at the situation.

"She's so pretty. This afternoon she drank a full four ounces with no trouble," I heard the nurse say behind me.

I didn't know what to say to her in response so I remained silent. My mind was all over the place and the last thing I wanted to do was have a conversation with a stranger. I guess she didn't get the memo because she continued.

"Hopefully if she keeps improving at this rate she can go home sooner than we thought. She's a little fighter. Must get it from you," the nurse smiled.

"How do you figure she gets it from me? You don't even know me," I told her with more attitude than I should have but she didn't seem fazed in the least.

The nurse was an older white lady who's name tag read Connie on it. She couldn't have been more than five feet tall with hair as white as snow and skin that resembled a raisin. She was a petite little thing but her eyes seemed to be filled with so much wisdom.

"Oh I been around a long time to pick up on things like this," she said as she moved around checking Kendal's vital signs. "I watched you and your wife in here the other night. You are a fighter because you haven't walked away yet. Somewhere deep down inside you feel that tugging at your heart to not only fight for your family but fight to get closer to God."

All I could do was look at this old woman in awe because she was hitting my situation dead on. No matter how mad I got at Chardonnay or stepped out on her there was something that wouldn't let me completely walk away. Even with her telling me she was done and putting my stuff out I just didn't feel like this was the end of us.

Looking down I felt Connie take my hand and place it inside of the incubator with the baby. Her little eyes were open and it was like she was looking right through me.

"The word of the Lord says in Isaiah fifty five and six, to seek the Lord while He can be found and call upon Him while He is near. Baby all you have to do is surrender it all to God and let Him fight this battle. The last thing you want to do is miss an opportunity to get in His face while you can. We don't know what the next minute holds so give it all to Him and let Him work it out."

It wasn't until she handed me a tissue that I realized that I was crying. What she said touched something in me but could I really leave my old ways behind me or make things work with my wife? Deep down I still had this feeling that Chardonnay was so adamant about us moving back to Savannah, not because of my infidelities but because she wanted to be closer to Gavon. That was just something that I couldn't get past.

Looking down I felt Kendal squeeze my finger with her little hand and although it wasn't tight it was just enough to open my eyes. If I couldn't be what I needed to be for Chardonnay then I had to at least try to be for the baby. That is if she was mine to begin with.

Chasiti

"I know she lyin!" Shenita yelled as Rochelle pulled her gun out and aimed it for my husband's head.

"Hey Chelle what you doing ma?" Danny asked her.

"So you the reason my son laying up in the hospital and his wife stepping out on him huh? I guess the God you serve didn't prepare you for this huh?"

"Man Chelle you already know how we get down. If you gone pull out on a G you better use it. But know that you won't make it out of here breathin' either," Reno told her.

Getting up from my seat at the table I calmly walked over to where Rochelle was standing and stood between her and Gavon.

"You bad? Let it rip then," I taunted. I didn't know if anyone else had picked up on it but Rochelle was all bark and no bite.

"Bae move out the way. She feeling some type of way about me let her do what she came to do," Gavon said trying to move me out of the way. He was now up on his feet but I wouldn't budge. There was no way that I was going to let any harm come to my man and if I had to step in front of a bullet for him then that's what I would do.

Rochelle stood there with her gun still trained on me and a smirk on her face.

"I see your old lady got more heart than you. Chardonnay was right when she told my son that you weren't really bout that life."

It was something about hearing Chardonnay's name and how she continues to keep my man's name in her mouth that tends to send me over the edge.

The laughter that came from my lips sounded like one of a mad woman. I guess it was fitting considering all of the hell that was going on around me concerning my family. Before anyone could react or realize what was going on I had hit Rochelle in her face as hard as I could and snatched the gun from her all in one swift motion.

Everybody in the room sounded like they were reciting Smokey's line from Friday when Craig knocked out Debo. There was so much pent up anger in me that began to surface that it took all of the men to pull me off of that woman.

"Okaaayyyy cuz got down with the hands! I underestimated you Chas," Shenita said excitedly. It would have been funny the way she was acting if things weren't so serious.

"Make sure you tell your daughter in law that you caught that beat down for her since you ready to body my man for her lying self! Gun ain't even loaded. Yea its time for yall to get out of the game cause fooling around with people like her gonna get yall killed. Who carries a gun with no bullets?" I said to Danny and Reno before leaving out of the room. I needed some air before I went in for round two.

Chardonnay

"Still up to your old tricks I see," I heard from
behind me. I felt like I had just closed my eyes when I was
awakened out of my sleep. Turning around I found myself
standing in a big open field where the grass was greener
than anything I had ever seen in my life. Not even the grass
in the rich neighborhoods could compare to this and it
seemed to go on forever.

"It's beautiful isn't it?"

I could hear the familiar voice but I didn't know
where it was coming from.

"Over here Chardonnay."

It was like she appeared out of nowhere sitting in a
rocking chair with her prayer cloth in her hand.

"Mama Jean?" Lord did I die and go to heaven?

"Baby you won't make it in with that nasty attitude
and bitter heart," she said as if she could read my mind.

"Still judging me I see. Must be out here cause God didn't let you in either," I sassed.

Instead of her usual comeback all she did was smile at me with a look of pity on her face that did something to me. Out of all the years I had known Mama Jean she had never looked so kind towards me of all people. All I ever got was attitude.

"Not judging honey being honest. See the only time someone feels like another is judging them is when they don't want to be held accountable for their actions. Jesus tells us that we should not judge others based on their appearance but judge righteously," she explained.

"Seems like to me you were always looking down on me," I said and put my head down. I didn't know what this feeling was that I was experiencing but it left me feeling uncovered. A feeling that I never liked feeling.

Getting up out of her chair I noticed that she no longer had a cane and she moved better than I had ever seen her move before.

"Did I like how you carried on? No but I never looked down on you. After dealing with you for years I finally came to the understanding that the way you handled life was only to mask the pain of what they did to you," she said reaching out for my hand at the same time I raised my head to look in her eyes.

"What are you talking about?" I asked. I had never told anyone about my past so there was no way that Mama Jean knew what she was talking about.

"God knows and sees all and sometimes He will give us just a glimpse into someone else's life so that we can help them. I wish He had given me insight before it got too bad but His timing is still perfect."

It felt like she was speaking in riddles or some kind of Morse code that she had with God and I wasn't getting at what she was talking about.

"I'm not understanding."

"Come," was all she said as she began to walk away. Not sure I wanted to be alone I said not another word and followed her until we reached a door. Now where this door in the middle of the field came from was beyond me but as soon as she opened it and we walked through I couldn't help but allow the tears to fall.

We were standing in the hospital room of a little girl. She was beaten so bad that her eyes were swollen shut and her little body was all bandaged up. There was a cast on her right arm and she had blisters from what looked like cigarette burns that covered at least seventy five percent of her upper body.

I walked over to her as Mama Jean stood by the window. I watched as the little girl's chest slowly rose and fell as the breathing machine did what it was designed to do. The beeping sound couldn't drown out the wail that escaped my mouth the moment I put her tiny hand in mine.

All of the memories of what led to that moment came rushing back to me like a flood as I looked down into the face of a ten year old me. I remembered all of the men that my mother allowed to run through me all because she blamed me for my father leaving us. He had walked out right before my fifth birthday and was never seen again.

For a while my mother held out hope that he would return and she was even more loving than she had been before but that all stopped one day when she saw him in out and about with his new family. Come to find out he felt like I wasn't his daughter and had gotten me tested behind my mother's back. As soon as he got the results that I indeed wasn't his flesh and blood he bounced leaving me with the woman who would wreak havoc in my life for years to come.

It was like she had gone from the warm, loving, supportive mother I had known to this monster that I had prayed God take me away from. And He almost did, literally.

The beatings, sexual abuse, drug use, and anything else my mother could use against me she used until I landed in that bed. By the grace of God one of the truancy officers from my school came by the house because I was out for the tenth consecutive day. When he got there he saw that the front door was wide open and there was a stench coming through the screen door. He called out to my mother and when he didn't get an answer he came in only to find her dead from an overdose and me barely holding on to life.

"Why didn't God take me too?" I asked out loud.

"Chardonnay you have a mighty work to do for the Kingdom of God. That's why you're still here baby."

far from loving on the outside but I guess her love for me on the inside prevailed and honestly I loved her too.

Getting up out of my bed I went to go handle my morning hygiene so that I could go and pump milk for my daughter. She had been eating up something lately and I knew her supply was getting low. I smiled at the thought of being the best mother I could be to her and I thanked God for waking me up before it got too late. The only thing I had left to fix was the issue between me, Gavon, and Chasiti as well as repairing my marriage. That is if they would all let me.

No More Thuggin

Alvin

To say that today has been an eventful day would be
an understatement. From the fight at the church to my son
getting a gun pulled on him was crazy. I knew that the devil
was out to get him but I had no idea the lengths that he
would go to get him off path. But just like a true soldier for
the Lord, my son was standing strong.

Now he has made some real stupid mistakes these
last few months from the looks of it but I knew his heart
was in the right place. All he wanted was be there for
everyone in their time of need and sometimes he left his
heart lead when he should have let the Spirit guide him. He
was still learning though as we all were and I knew that this
was only something that would make him stronger.

Throwing my keys on the table by the door I walked
into the house and kicked my shoes off. I had a long week
ahead of me and sleep was calling my name. Getting

comfortable on the couch I turned on the TV and grabbed the throw that was on the arm of the chair. As soon as I picked it up instantly my deceased wife's presence filled the room.

It had been years since I would see her in my dreams but each time I did it was like she was giving me just a little more strength to move forward. I would give anything to have her back with me but I knew that would never be possible. I thought of all of the fun times we had and even the hard times, but we got through them together.

Each and every time I closed my eyes while I was in lock up I would see her beautiful smiling face. I would never forget how her smile would reach her eyes or how hard she would roll them when she got upset with me. The way her hair smelled after she had just come from the salon and how she would rub my shoulders after a long day of work.

Danielle wasn't the normal housewife. She was deep in the streets with her brothers and no matter how many times I begged her to leave the streets alone she just couldn't. It wasn't until we had Gavon that she started to see the bigger picture and back away from that life but it was too late.

See we don't think about how the decisions we make in life can come back to haunt us even when we are ready to let that lifestyle go. She may have been ready to let that street life go but it wasn't ready to let her go. That harsh reality was right in my face the night I heard those gun shots and saw the woman I loved beyond words dying in her own blood pool. The only reason after all of these years that I had peace with her death was because I had the chance to help her repent before she took her last breath. It was hard that she was taken away from me and I was taken away from our son but knowing that she had given her life over to Christ before she left this earth was something I would forever cherish.

The sound of my phone ringing brought me out of my daze as I searched around on the couch for it. Looking at the screen I smiled in anticipation of hearing Marisa's voice.

"Hey beautiful," I greeted her.

"Hey handsome. What are you doing?" she asked.

"Just getting in from Gavon's circus," I told her.

"What circus?"

"Babe I would have to tell you in person it was so much. Just know it got real in the field."

"Real in the field? Boy who says that anymore?" she laughed and I couldn't help but to join in.

"Whatever you love it."

"You're right and I love you too," she said and I could hear the smile in her voice.

"And you know I love you more."

"So listen baby, I was thinking that we could get together with Gavon this weekend and sit down and talk to him together. I understand what he is feeling and I just feel like in order for us to move on without a hitch is to sit down and talk to him. I can't have the two of you fighting over me because eventually that will cause a rift between us. I see us in this thing for the long haul and in order for us to work this needs to happen."

I understood what she was saying as I listened to her but I was grown and if Gavon couldn't understand that then that would be his loss. I wasn't about to let Marisa get away from me only because of my son. That was not going to happen.

"And before you tell me how grown you are and that you are the father look at it from his side babe and try to really be understanding towards him. He lost his mother and grandmother, then he just got you back not too long ago after all these years and now here comes this new woman stepping in the place of where his mother used to be."

When she put it like that I started to understand exactly why he was feeling the way that he did. I was so blind to his feelings and thinking he was being selfish that I didn't look deeper into what he was really going through. I had dropped the ball and I needed to be the one to resolve this issue. As a man but more importantly as his father. He wasn't a little boy anymore so I had to come to him man to man.

"You're right Risa. I'll get everything set up," I told her.

"Ok love. Let me get back in here my break is almost over. I'll call you when I get home to let you know I made it in. I love you."

"I love you more," I said as I ended the call.

Closing my eyes once again and getting settled on the couch I got ready to let sleep overtake me.

No More Thuggin

"She's definitely the one," I heard my wife's voice say and at that moment all was well with the world.

Kendrick

"Wait tell me what happened again," I asked my mama as she paced the floor upset.

"I was in his house Ken. I wanted to dead that nigga but his wife jumped in my face."

My mama was fired up and here I was laying up in a motel bandaged up. I felt helpless but I was going to get at all of them in due time. I had no idea my mama was hanging with Gavon's peeps. As my mama puffed on her weed the door came flying open. I raised up from the bed because no one should have the key to my room and no one knew where I was.

"How did y'all find me?" My mama asked the two twins whom I assumed were Gavon's uncles.

"Ma you in our city. We know everything. You must be Kendrick?" one of the men said.

"Yea! Why? wassup?"

"Hold your horses youngin. Take the air out your chest. I'm not even the one to be playing with. Ask yo mama she know how we roll. I was just coming to make sure you was good Rochelle."

"I'm good Reno. I don't like the fact that I was put in that situation."

"I didn't know who your son was let alone him being married to our nephew's ex. You trying to put all the blame on us but who goes in a church to start a fight?" Dan asked.

"Look I don't know either of you but me and Gavon beef don't have anything to do you with you guys," I tried to explain.

"Youngin anything dealing with Gavon, his wife and their children got something to do with us."

"Hold on Reno let me ask this young cat something. Why you beefin with my nephew in the first place? Or is it cause you can't control your girl?"

I clenched my jaw because I was trying to stay calm. I was mad at both Gavon and Chardonnay. Her because she couldn't keep her legs closed and Gavon for not being man enough to tell me he was sleeping with my wife.

"Nah it ain't that I can't control my wife. Your nephew crossed boundaries that shouldn't have been crossed. I even went to him and he still lied to my face."

"Well I think both of y'all looking at it wrong. Now I'm willing to go and talk to my nephew and see if we can get this thing squashed but the first wrong move you make youngin it's over for you," Dan stated.

"I'm not letting my son go and talk to him by himself. I'm going too," my mama stated.

"Rochelle let your son be a man. You can't constantly keep babying him. He a married man and you round here trying to follow him and hold his hand. You need to get you a man," Reno said as they both walked out the door letting it slam closed.

"Mama how you get fooled up with some dudes like that?" I asked her after they left.

"Believe it or not they are some of the coolest dudes on this earth. And to be honest I don't want to lose my friendship with them because of this beef so when Dan call you go meet Gavon and work it out. Now where I need to go so I can see my grandbaby?"

"Mama ain't no need for you to go getting attached to this baby because she may not be mine," I told her.

"You let me be the judge of that. Y'all men kill me with that DNA mess."

Not wanting to argue any further I got myself together as I put my shoes on so I could head to the hospital with my mama. I made sure to keep my band on so I could get buzzed in a little quicker. The nurse was changing Kendal's diaper when we got there. When she finally noticed us she grabbed Kendal's little hand and waved it in our direction. I looked over at my mama and she was already putting her gown on and sanitizing her hands. I followed suit and we entered into the nursery together.

"She gained another pound. We are so proud of our little Kendal. Her mommy just fed her so she's full, changed and ready for her nap," the nurse stated.

My mama was sitting in the rocking chair gesturing for the nurse to bring her the baby. Because Kendal was still hooked up to certain machines the rocking chair had to be placed real close to the incubator. I gave Kendal another week and she would be in a regular crib.

"Ken Ken she looks just like Zana. This here is my grandbaby. I don't recommend you go through with the test. It's only going to hurt your marriage more," my mama said rubbing Kendal's little fingers.

"I hear you."

"This baby is going to need the both of y'all. You and Chardonnay are so stubborn. I knew when I first met her that she was going to be the one to tie your butt down because she was just as crazy as you. But seriously, you know how hard it is to take care of someone with special needs. I did my best with your sister but it was hard without y'all daddy. Now I need you to get with your wife and fix this."

It was crazy how just a few minutes ago my mother was poppin off at the mouth and now she was just as calm as a spring breeze. I guess a baby did that to some people. It could either bring them together or tear them apart.

"I didn't do anything wrong. She needs to be the one fixing it."

"I've tried Kendrick," Chardonnay said faintly behind me.

I turned around to look at my wife. She was beautiful but she carried the look of stress and worry on her face. She wore a bonnet on her head which was not like Chardonnay. Her appearance was everything to her.

"Listen y'all cannot do this in here. Arguing and bickering around Kendal is only going to stress her out. You don't want her to be sick because you guys can't get along. Gone somewhere and talk now, gone."

I got up and walked out. I took my stuff off as Chardonnay watched me. I desperately wanted to touch her but I didn't want her to reject me.

"Where you want to go?" I asked her.

"We can just go sit in the car if you want," she said with defeat in her voice.

"You hungry?"

"Nah I'm straight," she replied.

I knew my wife hadn't been eating. The pants she wore sagged in the back where she used to house one of her best assets. Looking at her in this condition let me know I had dropped the ball and I had to get her back right. We took the elevator down in silence. I glanced over at her and noticed she was still wearing her wedding ring. That made me feel like there was a second chance. She unlocked the door and we both climbed in. Again there was silence.

"So you said earlier that you been trying to get this thing right. How Char?"

"Kendrick you never listen to me. When you get mad at me you just shut me out and let someone else in. I've tried explaining that Kendal is yours, I've tried explaining that I've never cheated and you never give me the time to. Do I need to go on?"

"How am I supposed to know you've never cheated on me?"

"I'm not perfect Kendrick but when I married you I took it serious. Now I'm not going to sit here and lie and say I haven't thought about it. I almost kissed Gavon once but he takes his vows serious as well. I've never been with another man since being with you. Once I dogged Gavon like I did I vowed to never do it again to anyone else. I talked bad about him but truthfully he tried to do was make me a better person."

"See that's what makes me upset with you. You talk so highly of him now but when I first met you all you did was talk down on him. Are you still in love with him?"

"No I'm not. I guess I just want you to treat me like he treats his wife. Ken you got to open your eyes and see some of the damage you've caused us. The constant cheating made me feel insecure. I ran to Gavon with my problems because he was what I was familiar with here in Savannah. I just want to get this right. Our baby needs us, she's fighting so why can't we?"

To hear Chardonnay pour her heart out to me made me soft. It also made me realize that it was time to stop playing games and running. I had to man up and be the man that I was supposed to be over my household. I reached over and touched her face before I leaned over and kissed my wife passionately for the first time in a long time since we been married.

"I'm sorry ma. I really am. If you give me another chance I promise to work on me."

"I'll work on me as well," she flashed me her gorgeous smile.

We headed back up to check on our daughter hand in hand. I worked one problem out now it was time to man up and handle the next one.

No More Thuggin

Gavon

I squeezed Chasiti's thigh as she retwisted my hair. Lately she wasn't very talkative and I wanted to know what was going on.

"Gee do you think I'm too fat? I mean since having Lil' Gavon and getting on Depo I have gained a few more pounds. I was thinking about working out."

I turned around and looked at her, "Don't start tripping on me bae. You look good to me but I tell you what. If you want to work out I'll do it with you."

Seeing Chasiti smile made me smile. It was my job to make sure that her face never lost it and I wanted to make sure she stayed happy. Just as I turned back around Shenita came prancing through the living room with Jean'nae on her tail.

"Where y'all going?" I asked her.

"Eewww. Jean'nae we can't do nothing without your daddy wanting to know where we going huh? What we doing? If you must know we going to get us some huck a bucks and got to the shoot da chute."

"Tha who?" I frowned my face up at Shenita.

"Excuse me eeerrr. We are going to get a frozen kool aid cup and go to the playground if that's okay with you sir."

"All I'm saying cuz is speak English," we all laughed.

"I bet by the time I leave Jean'nae will know all the Nawlins' slang," Shenita said.

"Don't be teaching my baby that stuff."

"I think it's cute," Chasiti said high fiving Shenita.

"Ain't nothing cute bout that mess man."

As Shenita was walking out the door my uncles Reno and Dan were walking in. Mama Jean's house used to be the meet up spot but now that she was gone my house turned into the meet up spot. I was cool with it though because I loved my family.

"Nephew what it is?" Reno dapped me first followed by Dan.

"Wassup niece," Dan kissed my wife on the jaw.

"What brings y'all by," I asked as Chasiti kept twisting my hair.

"Well I talked to Rochelle and her son. I think the beef with y'all is a big misunderstanding. He's willing to sit and have a man to man talk with you if you willing," my uncle Dan said.

"I'm cool with it."

"I think we all need to talk," Chasiti said.

"Whoa wait now niece. Let the men talk then we'll bring everyone together. Rochelle still upset and I don't know what person Chardonnay is today so we got to do that at a later date," Reno said.

"Tell him he can pick the spot and I'll be there," I told my uncles.

They sat around with us for a little while longer and played with Lil Gee before heading out. After they left I decided to just spend some with my wife and son. My lil man was growing up so fast on me. I was playing airplane with him while Chasiti cooked dinner. His smile just like his big sister's was so contagious. He was a mixture of my mother and Mama Jean. My phone rung on the table and I took my son of my legs a secured him in my arms before I answered.

"Aye son. Are y'all home?" my Pops asked.

"Yea."

"I'm up the road. I got some company with me so don't be in your baller shorts and tank." My Pops said before hanging up

I hung up my end of the phone and took my son with me while I went to put some jeans and a shirt on. My

Pops was just like Mama Jean, if company was coming over she wanted you dressed and up.

"Chas you decent?" I yelled from the living room.

"Yea. Why?"

"Pops on the way with somebody."

Right after that came out my mouth I heard two car doors closing. I got up to open the door for them and behind my Pops was Marisa. I knew the time would come that we would have to talk but I didn't know if today was the day for me. I started to feel overwhelmed until Chasiti came and touched my hand that was holding the door knob real tight.

"Son I wanted you to meet Marisa and get to know her for yourself. So, Marisa this is my son Gavon. Gavon this is my lady Marisa."

My voice was caught in my throat. I knew what I wanted to say but it was like my tongue was stuck to the roof of my mouth.

"Hey y'all come on in," Chasiti broke the silence.

My wife led the way into our living room where Lil' Gavon was busy sitting in his bouncer. Marisa went straight for my son and I couldn't help to think how I wished it was my mother instead of her.

"Oh my goodness he has gotten big. Breast milk is always the best milk," she told Chasiti.

"Yes ma'am it is."

"Gavon it's nice to officially meet you," she said sitting next to my Pops.

"Likewise."

My Pops placed his hand on her leg and she relaxed a little. I guess she was just as nervous as I was.

"Well I guess you are wondering why we are here like this. I told Alvin that I totally understand your reservations when it comes to me. I too have been where you are. My dad died and I didn't want anyone to be around my mom but me. I couldn't see after a while that she was miserable because only my feelings meant anything to me at the time. I just want you to know that I will never try and take Danielle's place. Your dad still loves her deeply and I get it. From what he tells me she was a beautiful woman inside and out. I just want everyone to get along and I don't want to be the cause of any rift between you and Alvin," Marisa said.

I still couldn't really talk. It was good to hear that she wasn't coming to take my mama's place. I caught my Pops staring at me so I needed to say something I just didn't know what to say.

"Son I wanted y'all to meet because I'm planning to marry Marisa and move her in."

"When did you plan all this," I said finally finding my voice. The news that he was ready to get married came out of left field and I didn't know what to think. Obviously their relationship was deeper than I had assumed.

"Gavon, Marisa and I have been dating for some time now. We are both grown and we are tired of hiding because you can't seem to get out of your feelings."

"Al calm down. You're getting worked up about nothing," Marisa told my Pops.

"I'm cool with it. Whatever you wanna do. Do you Pops." I said nonchalantly and walked out.

"That's not the right attitude," Chas said coming in our room behind me.

"What? I'm cool."

"No you're not and you may think you are fooling them but you know you can't fool me."

"Chas they already talking marriage."

"And? Gee it doesn't matter when they get married you will think it's too soon. Until you accept this and let your mother rest you will be stuck in this same place. The point here is they included you in on it. They took time out of their day to come and sit and talk to you and all you gave was attitude. I can't let you keep on like this. Marisa seems to be good to and for your dad. He's happy, she looks happy so what's the problem?"

"I'm good! Congratulations to the both of them," I said before getting up and walking around to the other side of the bed.

"He'll come around," I heard Marisa say as I passed my open room door.

It was some things that I hadn't let go of yet. My mouth was saying it was cool but heart was feeling another way. I wish heaven had a phone so I could ask my mama how she was feeling about all of this. My phone started ringing and I could go for a distraction at the moment. Looking at the phone I already knew why they were calling.

"Wassup unc?"

"He said y'all can meet up in an hour at Lady and Sons."

***

I gave Kendrick time to get there before I popped up. I had enough going on and two meetings in one day was a bit much for me. I stepped out of my truck and took my shades off. Once inside I told the hostess who I was and followed her to the back. The restaurant was always crowded so he picked the perfect place. As I approached the table Kendrick stood up from his seat. He was dressed a little more casual then I was used to seeing.

"Thank you for meeting me here," Kendrick said holding his hand out. I took his hand and dapped him up. His other arm was still in a cast but his face had healed a little.

"You ever ate here? I heard it was good," he asked stalling.

"Come on Kendrick let's quit playing. Wassup?" I eyed him. I didn't know what the sudden change was but it made me nervous.

"Well first off I want to apologize for coming in you church starting a war. My beef with you is because of the time you were spending with my wife. You were in my house sneaking around. Now I guess my question to you is, did you sleep with my wife," Kendrick rubbed his chin hairs.

I chuckled, "The last you have to worry about is me sleeping with Chardonnay when I got a wife as fine as Chasiti at the house. The only reason I was at your house bruh, was to counsel your wife. She reached out to me and told me y'all was having problems. I suggested that we all meet but she felt that it wasn't good. Now I know why, she fed you and your mama a plateful of lies."

"Now wait I can't sit here and let you downplay my wife Gavon. I read some text message you wrote her as well. She wasn't the only one reaching out," Kendrick raised his eyebrow at me.

"Yea I'll admit I texted her when I was having issues with my Pops dating this new woman. Chardonnay is the only that I felt like understood me. Chasiti was riding with my daddy whereas your wife was making me feel like I was right. But to be honest I don't need advice from a 'yes man'. Chardonnay was telling me what I wanted to hear not what I needed to hear. And I'm not downplaying her by a long shot bruh. There is good in her, it's up to you to get it out of her. Everyone comes along that's for somebody. I wasn't the one for Chardonnay but evidently you are because she surely does love you. You got to change your ways too though Kendrick. How is your daughter?" I asked.

"She's doing good. She should be home soon. Did you know?"

"Did I know what?" I asked.

"My daughter would be sick."

"I did but it wasn't my place bruh. She was supposed to tell you."

Kendrick shook his head.

"Chardonnay and I decided that we needed to start over. Is there any way we can get the ladies to sit down and talk. I really need a man in my life to hold me accountable to my wife. And as crazy as it seems you bout the only one I can trust to lead me in that area."

I knew that it had to be God working this out and changing my heart towards this man and the situation. If we could get our wives on the same page I had no problem continuing to do what God led me to do.

"I got you bruh," I smiled at him.

Chasiti

I had just finished up the steak, potatoes, steamed broccoli, and chocolate cake that Gavon requested I cook. Since things were back on track with us I didn't see why I couldn't get that done for my man.

"Where Lil Gavon's shoes that match this outfit?" Shenita asked walking into the kitchen with my baby boy looking too cute in his black and white overalls and his hair in little twists. All I could do was shake my head because I knew that was all Gavon's doing. I told him he was too young to start getting locked up but he wasn't hearing it.

"You want his black or white Chucks?" I asked her.

"He can match my fly today. Where the black ones?"

I hadn't noticed that she was rocking the same colors with a pair of black Chuck Taylors too. Before I could answer her Jean'nae came flying around the corner looking just like the two of them.

"What you trying to do man? You taking Daddy babies out so you can use them to find you a man." Gavon entered the kitchen and began picking with Shenita.

"I don't need them to find something already found," she mumbled.

"What was that?"

"Come on Gee don't start yo mess. I'm not trying to get all riled up before bae gets here."

"WHAT?" he yelled. I tried my hardest not to laugh but I couldn't help it.

"What's so funny Chas?"

"Aww my boo mad?" I picked with him as I walked over to him and kissed his lips.

"Gone now bae. How she bringing some random dude to my house when my family is up in here. You know she don't know how to pick nobody."

"I heard that with yo ugly self!" Shenita yelled from the other room just as the doorbell rang.

"I'll get it and it better not be no knuckle head either," Gavon yelled back as he made his way to the door.

Peeking around the wall Shenita and I locked eyes because we were both thinking the same thing. As soon as Gavon opened the door he was about to flip!

"What's up Kareem?" Gavon said giving his assistant a brotherly hug.

"Chillin. You good?" he asked.

"I can't complain. Just getting ready to feed my face. What brings you by?"

Here it comes I thought as I glanced quickly in Shenita's direction. I swear this was the first time I had ever seen her nervous for as long as I've known her.

"You know I came to kick it with my girl and hang with the little people while you and First Lady spend some time." Kareem said with a smirk on his face. I held my breath and took a step back.

"Bet. You remember what I told you about how to make lil man's bottle right?" Gavon asked walking to the living room and grabbing the baby bag that I had prepared for this outing.

"Yeah. Jean'nae doesn't like bananas either and don't let her have juice until she finishes her food. If I forget anything I'm sure Nita will remember."

"Cool, cool. Y'all be careful and don't be out there making any of your own." Gavon laughed before waking back over to where I was standing with my mouth wide open.

"Baby close your mouth a fly may fly in it." He laughed knowingly.

I turned to look at Shenita and she looked like she was going to pass out at any moment but not before she found out what Gavon had going on.

"Umm…but…wait…hold on…how?" was all she could get out.

"Come on now who you think set this up?"

My head snapped around so quick you would have thought I was that little girl from the Exorcist causing both Gavon and Kareem to burst out in a fit of laughter.

"Look man when you came for Mama Jean's funeral Kareem was there. You know how she took to people in the hood when she saw something in them. He was feeling you as soon as he saw you but emotions were running high and he wasn't in a position to step to you right then. I picked up on it and let him know he had to get himself together before he acted on what he was feeling. I knew it was real how he looked at you because it was the same way I looked at my baby when I saw her," he said wrapping his arms around me causing me to blush.

"So why you ain't say nothing? Got me round hea' sneakin like I'm a lil boo," she said sucking her teeth and turning that attitude right back on.

All we could do was laugh as she finished putting on Jean'nae's other shoe while she mumbled under her breath and headed out the door.

"Make sure you back before dark," Gavon yelled out after her.

"Shut up!" she yelled as I went back to the kitchen.

"Why didn't you tell me?"

"Cause that's that man's business," he replied.

"Mmmm hmmm."

I was just about to go in on him to get the details when there was another knock at the door. After placing the plates and silverware on the table so that we could get ready to eat, our guests walked in behind Gavon. God knows if I wasn't saved all three of them would have gotten cut with the steak knife I had just sat down.

"Before you go off just hear me out ok," Gavon already knew it was about to be a situation.

Instead of responding I folded my arms across my chest and raised my left eyebrow.

"Kendrick and I met up a while back and worked things out. Things were a misunderstanding and we were able to move past it."

"We knew it was best to wait a while until the both of you calmed down before we met up. With Kendal getting out of the hospital and us trying to make sure she got the best care that she needed time just never seemed to be right until now," Kendrick spoke up. It was the first time that I noticed he was holding a carrier in his hand with the blanket thrown over the baby to protect it from the cool breeze.

God was really dealing with me and I was so outside of my comfort zone that I knew it had to be Him. He never worked in the areas we were the most comfortable in so that He could stretch us. Right now I didn't want to be stretched I wanted to be mad and petty but I had to still show the love of Christ towards them. It was painful but it had to be done.

"Gavon likes his steaks medium well. If you want yours well done I can throw it back on the grill for a few minutes since the coals are still hot," I said turning away to grab the sides. I could see Gavon smile and both Kendrick and Chardonnay release the breaths they were holding. I'm sure they thought I was about to go off but they better now that if I don't like what was said I could still let them things fly. Well not really but that's how 'gangsta' I was feeling.

Not too much was said while we ate so I knew that Gavon was trying to get a feel of how to move forward with this whole kum ba yah session he was trying to do. Every now and then Chardonnay and I would interject while the men talked like they weren't just fighting a few months ago. I could admit though, that from the way

Chardonnay was tending to their beautiful daughter Kendal I did see a change. I had to be careful though because the last time she 'changed' the heffa came wreaking havoc a second time. I had a long handle spoon in the drawer that had her name on it this time.

When she asked me if I wanted to hold the baby I decided to play nice because it wasn't the baby's fault. For some reason as soon as I got her the squirming she was doing along with the faint whining ceased as she studied my face.

"Hey angel cakes. What you doing all that moving for huh?" It was like she felt comfort in my arms and the smile she gave me broke away the anger I was feeling to both her mother and her father.

I was just getting ready to speak when Gavon's phone rang. Saved by the bell maybe?

"Marisa?" Gavon asked.

None of us could make out anything she was saying but from the way his disposition had changed we knew it wasn't good. I just prayed it had nothing to do with his father.

"We are on the way!"

Not caring what dinner was left untouched we all got up and started moving around getting the things we needed in order to leave the house.

"Baby what's wrong? Is Pops ok?"

"Yeah he's fine but my uncles and Kendrick' mom isn't," he said alarming Kendrick.

"What's wrong with my mama?"

"I don't know everything but Marisa said that she was just about to clock out when she saw people rushing my uncles in on a stretcher along with a woman. All she could get right away was that they had all been shot," he said as I locked the front door behind us.

"Come on yall ride with us. Since the kids are gone there is room.

Jumping into the family car I got the car started as fast as I could and peeled out of the driveway.

Immediately I started praying asking that God's will be done and He bring comfort to us all. This was about to be a trying time and I could feel it.

"Oh God Shenita."

Hitting the hands free button I placed a call to her. I knew how close she was to her dad and if anything happened to Reno she would lose it.

"Heyyyyy behbay!"

"Nita where are you?"

"Down to the seafood place. Guh you should see Jean'nae eating these mudbugs," she laughed.

"I need you to meet us at the hospital. We are on our way there now. Uncle Danny, Reno, and Kendrick's mother have been shot. That's all we know," I informed her.

Hearing the heart wrenching scream that came from her mouth caused me to be overwhelmed with sadness and I felt like the life was being slowly being sucked from me. Someone wasn't going to make it and I could feel it.

Not even ten minutes later we were pulling up and I dropped everybody off at the entrance while I went to park the car. As soon as I hopped out I saw Shenita and Kareem swerving into the lot.

"Is he ok?" she asked running up to me.

"I don't know yet I just parked. Gavon is in there."

"Go ahead First Lady I got the kids," Kareem said.

"Thank you," I told him as I grabbed Shenita's sweaty hand and rushed inside.

Before I could get to the nurses station to get info I spotted Gavon and Kendrick down the hallway speaking with a doctor and two officers so we rushed to them.

"Gavon what's going on?"

Both he and Kendrick looked at us with tears in our eyes. I knew it was serious and all I could pray and ask God for was for His perfect will to be done.

Gavon

Listening to the doctor tell me the condition of both of my uncles and Rochelle had me feeling like I was in a war zone. The injuries they sustained didn't look good for any of them. The moment I saw Chas and Shenita running over to us I knew this was going to be hard for them as well.

"Gavon what's going on?" Chasiti asked me.

"Looks like this may be some kids of retaliation." I didn't have the chance to explain everything before Marisa ran towards me from the back calling my name.

"Gavon! Gavon!"

Moving closer to her I waited for her to say something else but instead she reached for my hand and pulled me to the double doors she had just come out of.

"Danny is asking for you. I don't think he has a lot of time so we gotta hurry. Maybe he can tell us who did this and he only wants you," she said out of breath.

I felt a heaviness in my chest the moment I waked into the room and saw him laying on that gurney. Tubes and wires were coming from all over and the heart monitor was beating slowly.

"I'm here unc. Who did this to you?"

"Is it too late?" he said barely above a whisper.

Immediately I knew what he was asking.

"Nah Unc, you still got time. You ready to surrender?"

Nodding his head as a tear fell I went into prayer.

"Lord your son is ready to come home and wants to be welcomed into you loving arms. Unc do you believe that Jesus died for our sins?"

"Yes."

"Ask God for forgiveness of all of your sins."

"God please forgive me. For all of my wrongs. I'm sorry."

"Do you wish for Him to come into your heart and be your personal Savior?" I could hear the rhythmic beat of his heart get slower and slower and I knew he was slipping away.

"Do you Unc? Come on please."

"I do."

I breathed a sigh of relief as I told him, "Welcome Home Unc," right before he closed his eyes and the constant slow beeping changed to one long one.

Taking a few breaths as I held his hand and told him I loved him, I wiped my eyes and stood up. All of the doctors and nurses that were in there when I walked in all had tears falling down their faces too.

"Is that all that there is to it?" One of the nurses asked.

"That's it. The work begins after and it's not easy but it's worth it," I said as I walked out. I could tell that she was thinking about what she had just witnessed and I prayed for her to receive as well.

Leaving them to do whatever else they needed to his body I eased out of the door closing it behind me. Rounding the corner I ran right in to Uncle Reno, Shenita, Kendrick, Chardonnay, and his mother sitting in the hall waiting. The look on my face told them the news I was about to deliver wasn't good and Reno broke down.

"I knew it. I felt a part of me just be snatched away," he cried.

"What happened?" I asked. From the looks of it the two of them only had flesh wounds and would be ok after a little rest.

"My dirt finally caught up with me. Danny told me to get out but I didn't want to listen," he cried harder.

"We were getting gas to head back out of town. Danny kept saying he felt like something was about to go down so we needed to hurry. Right as we were about to pull off shots rang out lighting up the car. Because Danny was still on the outside about to get in he got wet up."

"Wait til I find out who did this!" Kendrick said as he paced the floor.

"This the problem right now! Someone does something to another person and then there has to be retaliation. It's too much. I've done my dirt and lost not only my brother but my Mama and sister behind this foolishness. I'm tired and as messed up as it sounds we deserve this and I ant keep going on like this," he said walking off towards where the police were filling out their statements.

I already knew what he had done when he turned his back to them placing his arms behind his back. We all looked on as the bewildered officers placed handcuffs around his thick wrists and read him his rights. For once, in

a long time, my uncle was manning up.

Epilogue

Alvin

I stood at the front of the church with my palms sweating as I watched my beautiful granddaughter and daughter-in-law walk down the aisle. My son stood to my left as Chasiti's grandfather stood to my right holding his bible while dressed in his robe. For a minute I never thought I would experience true love again like I had with Danielle but God is a God of second, third, and fourth chances and I was glad that He had given it to me.

The doors in the back of the room opened and I saw Marisa walk in being escorted by her father Leroy. I could tell she was just as nervous as I was but her eyes displayed no doubts. I did the best that I could to hold back my tears but it was no use. Gavon reached up and patted me on my back to comfort me.

"You got another real one old man," he said as he looked at my wife to be. I was so glad that he had finally come around and supported our relationship. It wasn't like I

needed his approval to move forward because I would have

no matter what he chose to do. But it made it easier and

more enjoyable to have his backing his old man.

"Who gives this woman away?" Rev asked.

"Her mother and I do," replied her father.

Stepping out of place I walked over to her and took

her hand in mine but not before giving her father a hug.

"Take care of my baby. God made her for just for

you."

"That's exactly what I plan on doing for the rest of

my life."

I listened as the ceremony went on but I was so

ready to get to the 'I do' part that I was fidgeting.

Squeezing my hand Marisa gave me a smile that let

me know she understood what I was feeling. Looking up

and back at the Reverend I knew I had to be trippin'. Right

behind him I could have sworn I saw Danielle and Mama

Jean standing there with the biggest smile possible on their

faces. It was then that I knew I could move on.

No More Thuggin

Chasiti

It was so hard to keep the tears at bay as I watched my father-in-law recite his vows. I didn't know how he was with his first wife but if this was any indication of how he treated her I knew Marisa would always be safe with him.

Looking around the church of familiar and unfamiliar family and friends I thanked God for all that he had done. There may have been many stumbling blocks before getting to this point and they were hard to deal with but with His help we all prevailed.

Once Danny passed and Reno went to jail I knew that I had to make sure that everything was right with my heart. That meant I had to face the one thing that I never had the energy for and that was to make peace with Chardonnay. We both realized that communication was key and had we just talked like adults and not acted out on our feelings then all of that could have been avoided. In the end though it made us both stronger women. Our faith was tested and after taking that test many times we finally passed.

Reno had done the right thing by turning himself in to the police for the murders of Mario and his father. That was a weight he no longer wanted to carry and he knew that if he didn't someone would end up getting hurt again. He wasn't willing to take that chance anymore. When Gavon went to visit him the first time he decided enough was enough and he too wanted to walk with Christ.

Its crazy how tragedies sometimes opened people's eyes. Being in ministry you hope that it doesn't take something like that for a change but it had to be harsh for some to learn.

Chardonnay and Kendrick were doing so well and had even joined the church and began working in it. Gavon and I decided that they had such a powerful testimony that they would be perfect to be over the marriage ministry, with supervision of course. They were still learning and growing so we were there to guide them.

Shenita and Kareem were a trip! She was the wild one and it was funny sometimes to see how he could calm her down with just a look of endearment. She had even joined and got to work with the children of the church.

Applause rang out bringing me back from my thoughts just as they were announced Mr. and Mrs. Alvin Cunningham. Following them out of the church to head to the reception hall Shenita and all of her loudness broke out.

"We gonna be next yall!" she said flashing a ring that I was just now noticing.

"Omg that's beautiful!" I squealed.

"Chas you so extra," she said.

"But you love me," I told her sticking my tongue out at her.

"I sure do and I will love you more for helping me plan it."

She didn't have to ask me twice. I looked around the room at all of the lives that were already changed and the ones that were still being changed and silently thanked God there was no more thuggin.

The End

Made in the USA
Columbia, SC
22 December 2018